THE
LOVERS
AND
THE LEAVERS

THE
LOVERS
AND
THE LEAVERS

ABEER Y. HOQUE

First published in 2014 by Bengal Lights Books, Dhaka

First published in hardback in India in 2015 by Fourth Estate
An imprint of HarperCollins *Publishers*

P-ISBN: 978-93-5177-209-5
E-ISBN: 978-93-5177-210-1

2 4 6 8 10 9 7 5 3 1

Abeer Y. Hoque asserts the moral right
to be identified as the author of this work.

This is a work of fiction and all characters and incidents
described in this book are the product of the author's
imagination. Any resemblance to actual persons,
living or dead, is entirely coincidental.

HarperCollins *Publishers*
A-75, Sector 57, Noida, Uttar Pradesh 201301, India
1 London Bridge Street, London, SE1 9GF, United Kingdom
Hazelton Lanes, 55 Avenue Road, Suite 2900, Toronto, Ontario M5R 3L2
and 1995 Markham Road, Scarborough, Ontario M1B 5M8, Canada
25 Ryde Road, Pymble, Sydney, NSW 2073, Australia
195 Broadway, New York, NY 10007, USA

Typeset in 11/14.5 GoudyOlSt BT by
R. Ajith Kumar

Printed and bound at
Thomson Press (India) Ltd

For the stylish, the stoic, the hungry,
and the inventive.

Contents

BEFORE YOU EAT

dawn, and she hasn't slept yet
under the mosquito net

rigged so many hours ago
reaching for water

she forces a sip
and air rushes down her throat

she stumbles to the bathroom
coughing catalysed

the light has begun
to sieve through frosted glass

enough to see the tangle
of braids, the dark of eyes

waiting for the morning
to arrive

Dawn, and electric lines slowly stamp themselves against the whitening sky. The dogs have awakened, and the air fills with their cries. After a particularly high-pitched yelp, the darwan shouts indistinctly. The barks die down for a moment, and the sound of his sweeping resumes, light and rough.

The season is cooling. A large woven basket by the kitchen door is filled with ivory heads of cauliflower, curved squash and pale-green string beans, all still muddy from their journey from Savar to Dhaka.

Komola wakes to the sound of the sweeping. In the semi-darkness, the blue flame of the pilot light is a familiar flicker. She rolls up her mat, sets the water to boil, and shuffles to the back door. The azan pierces the air in multiple conflicting streams of sound. She pulls her anchal over her head and bends to inspect the vegetables. A fat root of ginger falls to the floor. Where is the spinach, she wonders. Madam will surely ask.

She decides she will make fish tonight. Her specialty: ginger and lime sauce. The last time she made it, even Sir mentioned how good it was. She squats heavily, picks up the basket and takes it inside.

After breakfast, she clears the table and wipes down the bamboo placemats. She wishes they would go back to the plastic ones they used when Oyon and Tahsin were young. Those were much easier to clean as there were no slats for rice to get stuck between. Both boys are gone now, studying and working in America. She misses their presence in the house, especially Tahsin, whom she helped raise, she feels, practically on her own. The older son, Oyon, always frightened her with his tantrums, even though his anger was never directed towards her.

She knows Madam misses them too because, sometimes, she will talk to Komola about things she doesn't care about, like asking her what she's feeding the turtles in the garden fountain. Komola feeds the little creatures meat secretly, though Madam said to give them only carrots and cucumbers. They're not vegetarian, she's sure of it. The tiny flavoured pieces of beef are always gone when she looks.

Madam sometimes picks fights about inconsequential or silly things, like this morning. She scolded Komola for forgetting to put the box of cereal out for her friend who has recently come from America. Her friend wasn't even at the table, but Madam didn't care. She just wanted things done exactly as she asked.

Walking painfully down the staircase to the kitchen, she adjusts her sari and feels a small lump in the corner of the fabric. She unties the corner and finds fifty taka. It's the change from the money that Madam's friend gave her yesterday to buy medicine. She hurries to the guest room on the ground floor. Knocking, she hears a muffled answer and enters. The woman is standing by the mirror. She has obviously just woken up, and her hair is slipping out of ill-made braids. Despite her weight, she's quite beautiful. The plumpness suits her, glosses her skin, proportions her large warm eyes to her face.

'Nita Madam, here is the change from the money you gave me to get your medicine yesterday,' she says to her, holding out the folded brown note.

'I cannot take it.' The woman's voice is hoarse from coughing.

'No, you must.'

'It is nothing. Please, keep the money.'

'No, take it.'

'Next time you need medicine or something else, you can use it.'

'I always need medicine,' Komola says, sighing.

'Then you know you can use it. Now don't mention it anymore.'

'Okay, thank you,' Komola says, with the few English words she knows.

'You are welcome,' Nita Madam responds in

kind. She touches Komola's sari and continues in Bangla, 'I love this orange.'

Komola hesitates and then says, 'I didn't always wear colours. I used to wear white.'

'Why is that?'

'I got married when I was very young. My husband died only three months later.' She blinks as she remembers. 'I wore white for a long time. People would ask, why are you wearing white? So then I stopped.'

'I'm glad.'

'You are not married?' Komola asks despite her fear that she is overstepping her bounds. But Nita Madam seems different, more open than the other Bangladeshi ladies who have visited. And she seems not to mind the question.

'I was, long ago. I have a beautiful daughter, Ila. You'll meet her. She and I are moving to Dhaka. I'm here to find a place for us to live.'

'We have much in common.'

'Yes?' Nita Madam is rubbing the dark circles under her eyes.

'I also had a daughter, from my first marriage. But she died when she was only a little girl.'

'God help me,' Nita Madam says, her voice

cracking, 'I don't know what I would do if I did not have my Ila.'

'I left my village when it happened. I took a train to Dhaka. I left everyone, my little brother, Mintu, my older sister, July, my parents. I took nothing with me, only sticks of sugar cane to eat on the way.'

'It must have been very difficult.'

'It was. I lived with a family who beat me. The neighbours would hear me crying, and tell me to flee. But I was too afraid, so I stayed.'

'How long did you stay?'

'Five years? Eight years? Then I came here. I've been here twenty years. All this time, I have worked so hard. I have lived so long with so little.' Tears come to Komola's eyes. 'I am tired.'

Nita Madam touches her hand in sympathy.

'But one can always marry again,' Komola says, wiping her eyes with her anchal. 'My second husband is a very handsome man.'

'Ah, we have that in common too. My ex-husband is also handsome, but removed.' Nita Madam laughs bitterly. 'Besides, all the men my age are looking for much younger wives. What is there to do?'

Komola thinks the answer is clear, but she says it anyway. 'Don't give up hope.'

It is mid-afternoon by the time Komola finishes cooking the fish, and she is exhausted. She has outdone herself this time. Three whole fish, evenly blackened and sprinkled with coriander leaf and ginger shreds, are arranged on plates. The largest, the one she's most proud of, is lying on a cut-glass plate shaped like a fish that she found in the back of the cupboard. Each plate is ringed with round slices of cucumber alternating with red crescent wedges of tomato.

Her left knee won't bend now, after the hours of standing. Last week, it kept her awake the entire night. First, she tried the salve that someone had told her about. She had soaked a gamchha in a mysterious sticky paste, kerosene and hot water, and wrapped her leg in it. Last time, the concoction had made the pain go away, but this time, it turned her leg black and even stiffer. So she had to get tablets. The pain is getting worse each year. Sometimes, nothing works, not even the tablets. Madam made her go to a doctor last year, even though she didn't want to. The doctor said she had to stop eating sweets and lose weight. She doesn't understand what eating sweets has to do with her knees. She doesn't understand doctors.

The first time Komola visited a hospital was just after she married the second time. After the monsoon rains had ended, she had gone to her village to visit her parents. While washing clothes one morning, she ran out of water. The water in the pond was so dirty that no one used it anymore, although Komola still liked to wash her clothes on its banks. Leaving everything all twisted up on a flat black rock, she carried the bucket back to the well.

The tube well was the deepest in the village. The water was hard, clean and cold. She took hold of the long smooth handle and pulled it up and then pushed it down. A second later, water started gushing into the bucket. It was not as much effort as she remembered, but she had much more than childhood strength now. The rhythm was immediately familiar and she watched the reflection of the sky bounce and break on the surface of the water. But her hands were slippery with soap and, in a moment of carelessness, the handle of the pump flew out of her arms and hit her face, which swelled up immediately, distorting her features and making it impossible to see out of one eye. A ringing in her ears.

When the swelling didn't reduce after four days, she finally went to see the doctor in the nearby town. He bitterly rebuked her for not coming earlier and instructed her to buy some very costly medicine. What if the medicine didn't work? How was she to go back to the city like this? How would she work? And most urgently, what about her husband, who was to visit next week? She couldn't see him like this.

The pain was excruciating. It radiated from her cheek sideways, all the way to the back of her head. A cousin told her to pack a bag of ice and press it on her face. It was only after doing this for a few days that the swelling started to go down. Sometimes, she imagines she can still feel the distension almost two years later. She can still hear the ringing.

The late afternoon light is stealing out through the windows of the kitchen. This house, full of its comforts and amenities, feels like a place from which all sound has vanished. And here she is, standing in a dirty kitchen she now has to clean, tired and alone.

When the phone rings just then, it is as

startling as a slap. It's her husband, calling from his mobile phone shop in Mymensingh. He lives there with his first wife and his children. Komola is his second wife, the one he married for love.

His first wife knows of Komola. She's known since their love began, but she doesn't say anything. Only in the beginning, the wife told him that he must not leave her, that it would malign her. So he only comes to Dhaka every few months. Mymensingh is far, half a day by bus.

Her shock at the ringing of the phone is overcome by joy and then replaced with resentment, all in the seconds it takes to answer. He doesn't notice her mood for a few minutes, and then finally asks her what the matter is. Her husband is a happy man. She knows she's lucky for having found love and laughter so late in life. He laughs all the time, sometimes even when she's upset. This time though, he doesn't laugh.

'Jaan, my heart, are you crying?' he asks in surprise.

'It's because you're not here,' she says as evenly as she can.

'I don't know what to tell you…' he says gently. She hears something else in his voice.

Irritation? Defensiveness? She doesn't know, but it only upsets her further.

'Why is it that you can call me any time?' she asks plaintively. 'A time like this, like today, when I am so busy. Yet I can always talk. But when I call you sometimes, it's not the right time.'

'If you are too busy to talk, just tell me. I can go,' he says easily.

'That's not what I meant.'

'Then what did you mean?'

'All I want is for you to come here. Then I'd be at peace.'

'At peace, my love? You are not at war, are you?' He is laughing again.

'I don't know,' she says petulantly, although she's feeling better in spite of herself.

'Anyway, if you must know, I am coming tonight. I was going to surprise you, but since you are in such a state, I am telling you now.'

She is so happy she can barely breathe. Instead, she finds herself admonishing him, 'You cannot laugh as loud as last time. I am sure Madam and Sir heard something.'

'What? Married people can't laugh?' he says teasingly.

'Yes, but they don't know about your visits. I know they would not like such a thing.'

Sometimes, she feels worse after she talks with him on the phone, even though the phone brings his voice so close. There is something wrong with the sound, something flat and electric, something that reminds her, even if she closes her eyes, that it's not real, that he's not there. All she wants is for her beloved to be near. It's not about jewellery, or sweets at a wedding feast, or flowers in her hair. It's just the feeling of standing beside someone you love.

Unlike her first wedding, her second wedding ceremony had not been much of an affair. She had gone to her village only to see her parents, and he had come to visit two days later. The people in her village had said that it was not right that they stay together and not be married. So they got married. She wore a pink sari, and as much jewellery as her family owned. Much to her chagrin, they had not fed anyone as per tradition. He had said they didn't have enough money. Perhaps when she saves up a little more money, she can still have a little feast for her family and friends.

At dusk, she bathes and dresses in her best

sari, a bright printed cotton with blue and yellow flowers. She carefully applies kohl around the edges of her eyes, and combs her hair. Though not so thick anymore, her hair is still long and dyed a jet black. He will be here very late, but she wants to be ready, even though she knows she has work yet to do. The bulk of it is done. She only has to clear and clean. Then she can wait for him.

Her conversation with Nita Madam earlier that day echoes in her head. It has been so long since she had spoken with someone other than her husband.

'It's love,' Komola had told her. 'We have love.'

Nita Madam had smiled.

'You know when you're hungry?' Komola cupped her right hand in a habitual motion. 'You want to eat some rice.'

'Yes.'

'Well, before you eat, there is love. It comes even before your hunger.'

'It's true,' Nita Madam had said, still smiling. 'God forgive us, but it's true.'

'Isn't that true?' she had asked again.

'Akdom.' Absolutely.

In the night, her husband will call her from his phone, as he always does, from outside the gate,

even though the darwan knows him and would
let him in. She will ask him to enter, and he will
meet her in the dark to the side of the garden.
She will take him round to the back of the house,
inside and up the stairs to her room. Before she
locks the door, she will ask him if he's hungry. If
he is, she will bring him the leftovers. If not, she
will swing the heavy metal loop of the padlock
into place and close it, so that no one can come in
and find them. She will switch off the electric light
to save power, and light the candle. Only then,
sitting next to him on the woven mat from her
childhood home, will she feel her insides unwind.

The candle will eventually gutter, long after
their breath turns from laughter to sleep. The
white bougainvillea she picked from the garden
at dusk will drape its leaves around the sides of
the cracked drinking glass. The gas-fired stove
will remain burning, slowly spreading into the
light of the morning.

THE STRAIGHT PATH

oh my soft-skinned sharp-tongued girl
how does your garden grow?
with violet diversions and careless replies
and clairvoyance planted so

oh you're crooked in straight disguise
(what would I do for a kiss?)
reckless, racing, I make my escape
your flowers spilling from my lips

'Eight per cent?' Ila's voice is hoarse, scornful, confident. She laughs and crosses her legs. Her buxom body curves like a wink. 'They're joking, right?'

'Well, it says in the article that women tend to understate their sexual exploits, and men overstate...' Rox says, looking up from the *Baltimore Gazette* at her old friend. She finds it hard to look away sometimes. Ila has always been striking. When she was younger, the punk haircuts and goth makeup only highlighted her large eyes, so like her mother's. Now she's returned from Bangladesh all grown up and more beautiful than ever. She's also walking the straight path after years of stylish hedonism. This includes a Bangladeshi husband with exceptional educational and social pedigrees, and although she's currently wearing Western dress, Ila has a closet full of saris she can tie with as much grace as the next aunty.

'Yeah, that makes sense, but what's the percentage for married women cheating now?' Ila is clearly engaged.

Rox is amused, wondering if Ila's enthusiasm speaks of something real. She continues reading, 'Thirteen per cent of married women in America cheat on their spouse, up from eight per cent a decade ago. But the men's percentage hasn't changed in years: twenty-two per cent.'

'That's a big fat lie too. Guys must be well over fifty per cent.' Ila pulls back her henna-streaked hair from her face and lets it go. 'Here, let me read the article.'

When they were seniors in high school, just before Ila left for Bangladesh, she came on to Rox. They were drunk and had just stumbled out of a bar in the Inner Harbor, south of downtown, where a man, believably named Bam, had bought them drinks all night in return for half-smiles and mumbled thanks. Rox stood by Ila's mother's Mercedes parked thoughtlessly in the shadow of the grimly peeling wharves while Ila fumbled for her keys.

'Let me drive,' Rox had said. She was perhaps three-fourths of a rum and coke less drunk than Ila was.

'Are you kidding? This is my mother's fancy car. I have to take the blame if something happens. She usually never lets me drive it. It's just that the station wagon is at the mechanic's, and also, she's away.'

Ila was wearing a tiny leather skirt and a gauzy top, her bare legs golden in the light of the lone street lamp. Rox had on an equally ambitious skirt, in green cotton. They drove off at ten miles an hour into the suburbs, smoke from Ila's cigarette trailing behind them, Sade mourning from the speakers. The moon was so bright that their headlights seemed unnecessary, and after their tenth laughing fit, Ila stopped the car by some gnarled pine trees and leaned across the butter-coloured seats towards Rox.

Rox flops across her narrow twin bed and looks around. Her old lamp-lit bedroom is at once familiar and strange, as if all that's left of the person who lived here is her aura, outlined by the books heaped everywhere. From *The*

Velveteen Rabbit inscribed with her mother's slanted script on her fifth birthday to *The Delta of Venus*, her college boyfriend Arul's parting gift, and everything in between.

Firoz bursts into the room, and she jumps up in equal glee. He's her favourite of all the kids in her parents' circle of friends. Last time they'd met, almost a year ago, he was jubilant at finally having grown infinitesimally taller than her and insisted on a photograph for evidence. Now, he's seventeen and unmistakably taller, though his narrow frame has yet to fill in. He has been stronger for years though, as she found out during an arm-wrestling match a couple of years ago. Firoz is athletic and reckless, so he is hardly ever without an injury or two. Their first bonding moment was when he was nine and had an especially bad scrape on his knee. Rox, home on fall break, was the only one who consented to a viewing and then offered to throw ball with him. She wonders what Firoz will be like in college. He's silly and subversive and sharp. Perfect first-love material.

Ila looks up to smile hello and continues reading. Rox pushes Ila's legs aside and sits, pulling Firoz down beside her.

'Tell me. What news comes from the seventeen-year-old world?'

'Boring news, Roxanne apa,' he says, slyly using the term of deference that she's asked him not to use. 'Nothing ever happens.'

'Not true. You must have a girlfriend now.'

'Who told you that? Your brother? Did he tell you about last weekend too?'

'No, tell me.' She is always surprised at Firoz's willingness to divulge. There seems to be no end to the secrets in the Baltimore Bangladeshi community, and with good reason, given the backbiting backlash that accompanies the slightest slights. There's danger even though she is the black-sheep-hip-older-sister type.

As Firoz launches into his story, Ila lowers the paper and glances at Rox, amused. She knows Rox thinks Firoz is cute, though she doesn't see it herself. Most people in the community wouldn't. Firoz is automatically excluded from the good-looking category because of his dark skin. His careless demeanour and habit of breaking things, including himself, doesn't help. On the other hand, Qasim, another family friend's son who is also seventeen, is much sighed over by mothers and daughters alike. His condensed-milk complexion and smooth voice gets them every time. Rox would want to see how Qasim fared in college too, but Firoz is the one she'd call to climb walls at midnight.

There's a knock on the door.

'Come in!' Rox calls, and the door swings open. Her mother is standing there with Ila's daughter in her arms. Ila stretches out her arms, and the toddler struggles out of Rox's mother's grasp and tumbles desperately towards Ila.

'She got a little panicky downstairs,' says Rox's mother. Rox knows she's wishing that this were her own daughter, elegantly reclining with her grandchild. Instead, her irrationally single offspring is shamelessly flirting with a boy almost a decade younger. Of course, Rox's intentions in this regard are so far removed from the acceptable that they would not even occur to her mother. Her arm draped around Firoz's neck remains utterly guileless.

'Where's my husband? I left her with him,' Ila says, the barest edge in her voice.

'Neechay. He's watching the game, with everyone else,' Rox's mother says indulgently. 'Dinner is ready. Come down, OK?'

The smell of richly spiced meat floats into the

room and Rox is instantly hungry. Her stomach growls. Firoz laughs and pats her midriff, and she is reluctantly and unevenly aroused.

$\backsim$

'You would be doing the entire male species a favour,' Raza says just before he shovels a massive amount of rice into his mouth with chopsticks. He chews contentedly, his hazel eyes fixed on Rox. They're in Raza's favourite dive Chinese restaurant in New York City. Even though she's lived in New York longer, Raza always seems to know more of the hole-in-the-wall gems.

It's been a few weeks since Rox's mother's dinner party, and she's debriefing him on the Bangladesh community gossip. Raza is disconnected from the usual scandal grapevines because of his own scandalous family. His mother had married an American and then divorced him when Raza and Juthi, his sister, were teenagers. When his sister disappeared amidst rumours of drug addiction, their family's contact with the community became even more limited. But because their mothers teach at the same local college and remained friends, Raza and

Rox also stayed in touch. She doesn't see him very often, but when they do meet, they always have a good time. He's different from most other Bangladeshi boys she knows, and not just because he studied art in college. He is a staunch feminist, and although he uses stereotypes and makes outrageous declarations, underneath the stockbroker machismo, he is fair, self-deprecating, and likes a good conversation more than anything.

'How do you figure I'd be doing the *entire* male species a favour?' Rox is curious. Raza's theories usually start with over-the-top statements like these, but they are always entertaining.

He pincers a shrimp dumpling and flicks his hair off his forehead. 'Just think, if you fucked this seventeen-year-old kid, he would have a story to tell a hundred of his closest friends about getting laid by an older woman, and those friends would tell their friends, and you'd basically be providing masturbation fodder for thousands of guys.'

She starts laughing, but before she can respond, the waiter approaches their table to refill their water glasses. She glances over to the entrance where there appears to be a full bar. 'Could I get a margarita with salt, on the rocks?'

He hesitates and then pulls out a pad of paper.

'Our bartender is not here. But tell me what is in it, and I will make you one.'

She looks at Raza, who shakes his head. She shrugs and turns back to the waiter, 'Tequila, triple sec—'

'Lime juice...' Raza interjects.

'Anyway, I couldn't sleep with Firoz,' she hisses amiably as the waiter hurries off. 'Impossible. He's just a teenager. It just couldn't happen. Unless everything were different. Like we were in some foreign country and no one would ever find out.'

'Roxanne, I think you're the first person ever to have ordered a margarita in this restaurant,' Raza says, distracted by the waiter's motions behind the bar. He looks at the gleaming watch on his wrist. 'I'm going to time how long it takes him.'

'I know, I know. It's going to suck. But I don't want to lose my happy hour buzz.'

'So are you going to fuck him?'

'Stop using that word,' she says, rolling her eyes, though it's more his question than his language that's making her uncomfortable. Despite the Bangladeshi community's subtle but certain shunning of his broken family, Raza does not seem aware of, let alone concerned with its various negative dispositions and reactions.

'I used to fantasize about fu—, I mean, having sex with an older woman when I was a teenager.' He pauses, and then adds curiously, 'Are you afraid you'd be corrupting him?'

'No, not at all. The experience would probably help him more than hurt him,' she says in amusement.

'You know, you couldn't reverse the genders and get away with it.' He points a chopstick at her, pushing up his impeccably folded shirtsleeves. Raza has always dressed with style, even before the bankrolls began funding his wardrobe. In a funny way, he had come into his own when his sister had gone away. One time in high school, he had showed up at a dinner party in ripped jeans, bottle-green eyeglasses, and platinum streaks in his hair. All the uncles and aunties thought he was crazy. She and Ila had thought he was to-die-for cool.

'Very true.'

The waiter returns with her drink in a tiny tumbler, no salt. They both eye it dubiously. Rox drinks gingerly.

'Not bad. But it needs more lime juice. Try it.' She is so used to pinching salt off the rim and licking her fingers that she picks at the rim reflexively before handing Raza the glass.

He reluctantly takes a sip. 'Oh, I kind of like it, actually. But back to the topic – are you going to do it?'

'I told you, no way in hell. It's just fun to think about.'

'Fine. I'll just have to tell a little white lie when I tell a hundred of my friends this story.'

'Of course,' she laughs.

∽

The next time Rox sees Firoz, it actually is in another country. In Canada, at a Bangladeshi convention in Montreal. They're both accompanied by their parents, as well as sibling-less, because both their brothers have managed to pull off superior excuses. Firoz's last high school summer job is over and he has a week before he starts at University of Maryland, Rox's old alma mater. Rox's parents bought her ticket from New York, eliminating her strongest excuse about funds. She works at a nonprofit firm, which leaves her very little discretionary income. She knows her parents are hoping she'll meet a suitable boy, though the chances of that are slim, given that the men in her age group already seem to have a wife in tow.

'You'll be bored out of your mind, Rox,' Ila had told her when she had called her up last week.

'I know that already, but my parents are dying to go, and they really want me to come along. Any chance you might make it?'

'My daughter's not feeling well, but even if she were, I can't take more time off work. We went to Disneyland just last month. Sorry, babe.'

She even calls Raza although she can't really imagine him at this sort of an event. Predictably, he shouts with laughter when she mentions it.

'Canada? Rox, you're funny. Anyway, I have a way better idea. My old roommate from Harvard just moved to New York and we're having an all-out weekend. You remember Sailan. The Indian Spanish one. You thought he was hot, didn't you?'

'Um, you mean the totally arrogant one who thought he was God's gift?'

'If I remember correctly, it didn't stop you from looking God's gift in the pants. No matter you had a boyfriend who was madly in love with you.'

'Ok, fine, he *was* hot. And Arul was my *ex*-boyfriend then,' Rox protests.

'Barely,' Raza says.

She hangs up on him, laughing. It's probably better that Raza can't come to the convention.

There are too many dangers in that proposition. She can just see him at the convention, making eyes at all the aunties, arguing with the uncles about religion, his thumb circling the hip flask in his pocket.

So she and Firoz end up attending the various lectures and events alone. It seems there are more single people her age than she had expected, though probably not as many as her parents had hoped. And she hasn't seen any yet who looked cool enough to approach cold.

After a day of interminable lectures about the economic philosophies and political goals of the North American–Bangladeshi diaspora, Rox gives in to Firoz's request that they attend the Youth Issues meeting. It might be interesting to see what kids are worried about these days. When she was in college, these discussions were at such a nascent stage that the parents insisted on adult chaperones in the room, which made for an exceedingly tense and toothless debate. It seems things are different now. The dress code includes articles of clothing that she would have had to hide when her parents came to visit her at university. Other than the earnest-looking moderator who appears to be college age, there are no adults of the usual parental variety.

Firoz has his eyes full. The room is packed with fashionable silk-haired teenage waifs who tread the fine line between confidence and snobbery, managing to look bored and flirty at the same time. A particularly made-up teenager, whose ruched shirt is covered with dusty glitter, starts a discussion with a bomb of an opening line.

'What's worse for Bangladeshis – dating a Hindu, or a Jew?'

Good question. In Rox's mostly secret and often tumultuous dating life, she thinks it was hardest on her parents when she was dating a Hindu, even though she had thought it would be easier. After they sobbed over the irreverent Catholic white boy and then the sexy self-made Jew, she thought for sure the articulate Indian activist, who knew all the culinary and cultural intricacies, would go over well. She was wrong. Instead, she heard story after story describing in personal and emotional detail, the ancient and still powerful Hindu–Muslim divide. And that was just her mother.

Through her mother's earnest trembling voice, Rox pictured with absolute clarity her grandmother as a little girl, standing in a classroom in Bangladesh, head bowed, as her Hindu teacher hit her with her own notebook because the teacher had mistakenly taken it home instead of marking it and giving it back right away. Why hadn't the Muslim girl reminded the teacher to return her book before she went home? The teacher had had to cleanse her house with cow dung and do multiple pujas because her home had been tainted by a Muslim's property.

Of course, at the time, Rox had knelt to the occasion and raised her voice about past griefs from another generation not being relevant to the present. How neither Arul nor she had deep-rooted and intangible hatreds of each other's religious backgrounds. When her father entered the debate, they took it to another level – a furious and elevated intellectual debate that culminated in the same despairing lament from each one of them: you don't understand or respect me.

Definitely Hindus. Perhaps things aren't as different for kids from when she was younger.

'Let's go,' Firoz whispers, taking her elbow, as the conversation starts to digress into a litany of excuses and lies used to sidetrack and mislead strict Bangladeshi Muslim parents.

'Where are we going?' she asks as they break

into a run down the hideous flower-carpeted hallway of the Holiday Inn. Massive purple roses and green stems twist below their feet.

'You'll see!' he calls, pushing open a side exit door that leads into a small courtyard. When she enters the courtyard, she can hardly see anything. It's dark and cloudy, and the only lights are from a balcony above.

'Where are you?' she whispers.

'Up here.'

Firoz is scaling a metal trellis half wrapped in ivy. He pulls himself over the balcony, silhouetted by ambient lamplight. Rox smiles, remembering her unconscious prediction about climbing walls at midnight with him.

'I think you forgot that I'm wearing a sari.' The gem she's wearing is one of her mother's best, an antique royal-blue silk from when she first got married. Even more precious to Rox is the petticoat she always wears with saris. It's too short and her mother always complains about its threadbare condition, but it was her grandmother's and wearing it makes her feel closer to her.

'Roxanne…' Firoz's groan floats down from above.

She sighs, hikes up the sari carefully, and starts climbing an empty part of the trellis, praying that nothing will catch on the metallic threads of the fabric. She gets to the balcony seemingly unscathed and realizes that they have broken into the hotel's VIP spa and pool area. It's obviously locked up for the night, but only recently because the hot tub is still quietly steaming. Firoz starts to peel off his clothes as he heads towards the pool. She watches his body emerge from under a Nehru-collared red kurta, and the jeans that his mother could not dissuade him from wearing to the convention. He throws his clothes onto a lounge chair and looks at her.

'Come on.' He adjusts his boxers.

'No. You go ahead.' Rox settles into a lounge chair and kicks off her sandals. She hates the girly shoes that her mother makes her wear to desi functions. Despite the fact that her mother is almost half a foot shorter than she is, their feet are almost the same size. This means that Rox's more practical wedge shoes can immediately be axed for a strappier number. These binding blue stilettos were brought along with the sari to Montreal. There's a gold pair matched with a black and gold sari in their hotel room for tomorrow's events.

'Are you sure?' Firoz says, approaching her.

'Absolutely.'

'Too bad,' he says as he breaks into a run and hauls her off the chair in one swift, heart-thumping fireman's move. 'Because you're going in one way or another.'

'Wait! Wait! I'll go in! Just let me take this off – it's Amma's sari – I can't ruin it, please!'

He puts her down gently on the rough concrete and hovers while she hurriedly unwraps six glittering yards of midnight-blue from her body. She is still unbuttoning the matching blouse when he picks her up again and runs towards the pool. As he jumps off the ledge over the dark still water, she struggles out of the blouse and throws it as far as she can.

When they surface, Rox is wearing only a petticoat and a bra. She looks over to the side and sees her blouse and sari, lying in two glimmering heaps at the edge of the pool, inches but safely away from the rippling water. Firoz is laughing from the shallow end. He climbs out and runs dripping to the diving board. The board sounds a metallic reverberation as he cannonballs off its edge.

The wind has picked up and fat silver clouds are splitting and tearing across the sky.

Her grandmother's petticoat swirls palely and transparently about her legs. Firoz appears next to her, his breath quick, his teeth gleaming in the darkness.

'Isn't this much better?' he asks, his legs brushing briefly against hers.

'Than listening to how US political districting affects the Bangladeshi population here? Yes. This is much better.' Rox wonders where her mother is, if dinner has been served yet, what the hell she's doing.

Firoz leans over towards her and pushes a strand of hair from her cheek, his finger dragging unbearably across her face. She leans away from him and hooks her feet around his waist, stretching out on her back. His skin feels like liquid, like silk. He starts a breaststroke across the pool, pulling her behind him. The water sloshes in her ears. As they get to the deep end, she feels his hands taking hold of her feet as he dives in. She inhales, a quick deep breath, and sinks into the wet darkness.

ALO

she sits on the bed
as the rain counts out
the minutes of her life
on the tin roof
dhip dhap

she ignores the call
her husband in hunger
her sons in thirst
she in thrall
to what's coming
dhip dhap

a teasing wind
steps through the grilled window
furls the pages
of the calendars on the wall
obsolete all
2005 falls back with a slap
1998 caresses '99
dhip dhap

she undoes the khopa
at the back of her head
in a lightning crackle
crow black hair
loose to the air
and now
the real rains begin
dhip dhap

My name is Alo. I am six and it is the rainy season. Nobody knows, but I can guess what people are going to say, so I don't have to listen most of the time. Sometimes, when I have something else I want to do, I will jump into the future and answer from there. That way, I can finish talking sooner and go play in the rice paddy field with my goat, Kishmish. There's lots of water in the fields and the stalks are sharp and green. I like the sound it makes when I walk in it, the swirl of the water around my ankles, the mud sticking, sucking between my toes.

Abba is telling me about Kurbani Eid. About Prophet Ibrahim and how he is going to sacrifice his son for God. But God stops him before he does it. He puts a ram under Ibrahim's falling knife instead. That's why we celebrate Kurbani Eid by sacrificing an animal, Abba says, because of Ibrahim's faith. I hate it. I hate it because Abba is going to slaughter my goat even though he knows I'm afraid of blood. He says I shouldn't be, that it will be an honour for Kishmish, but I don't want him to die.

I want to stop thinking about blood, so I look ahead to see what Abba is going to say. He's going to talk about how blood makes us all the same.

A picture of Abba's body merging into mine comes into my mind. It's not scary, but I don't understand it.

'We're not the same,' I shout as I run out of the house. I don't wait to hear what Abba says. I never wait. It's Abba who told me that looking backwards is only for old people.

Sometimes, when I jump ahead into the future, I see the wrong answer. But that doesn't happen very often and no one seems to notice anyway. Ammu knows when I'm doing it. When I look ahead with her, she always stops what she's doing and watches me. When I get it right, she claps her hands and laughs, her thin bangles clinking. She leans down and kisses me on the forehead and whispers, 'Now, run out and play, my little prophet.'

Joy is my older brother. He is seven and just started class one. Ammu sewed his uniform at night after dinner. Abba could have done it because he's a weaver, but he won't because that's Ammu's work. It took her a month because she's not very good at sewing. Abba says she's not very good at many things, only at talking and wasting time. She only laughs when he says this. Her hair is coiled into a shiny khopa at the back of her head. She likes to shake the bun loose and retie it. Abba always falls silent when she does this. I wonder if he can hear the same thing, the spark and hiss of the strands swishing against each other.

Ammu says she'll make my uniform too, but that I have to be good or else I won't get to go to a good school like Joy. I don't want to go to school. Not if Joy will be there. He always finds reasons to beat me. When he hits me on my head, it hurts so much I can't even cry. I just sit on the cool dirt floor of the compound and try to push the buzzing out of my body in short bursts. Push, I think. Go.

I don't think I'm making any sound, but Ammu runs in and asks me what's wrong. I can't both push and talk and so I don't say anything.

'Just let Alo be,' Abba says from the doorway, retying his blue-check lungi around his waist. 'You make him weak with all your fussing.' He turns away and bumps into Joy. 'What are you doing here?' he asks.

'Kissuna,' Joy says. Nothing.

'Then go to bed.'

'But I have homework,' Joy says. He loves saying that he has homework. Abba always leaves him alone then. Ammu can't read, but still, she sits with Joy every night, looking over his shoulder by the hurricane lamp light. She says if he studies hard, he can become like her great-grandfather who used to be the school headmaster. But Joy doesn't want to be headmaster. He wants to be a police inspector. Then he can beat up anyone, even in front of Abba and Ammu. He pretends to load and cock a gun at me when he thinks I'm being bad. I've seen the superintendent cock his pistol so I know he's doing it wrong, but I run away anyway.

In the middle of my pushing and breathing, I see Abba and Ammu walking away from me, Ammu's black burqa billowing around her. I gather my strength, stuff it back small and tight into my body, and I call, 'Don't go! Don't leave me!'

When the sound clears, like the ripples in the paddy water, I realize that they aren't going anywhere. They are just standing there, looking at me. I've jumped into the future wrong. Ammu isn't wearing her burqa either. She's wearing her green sari.

In the morning, I wake up with a buzzing sound in my ears. I run to find Ammu but she's gone to the market. Abba is in the field. I can see Kishmish nuzzling up to him, not knowing that Abba is going to kill him in two days. I jump over the doorsill to avoid stepping on the flowers Ammu painted on it for a wedding.

As I come closer to the field, the buzzing dies down, and the paddy voices come. There's the noise of the insects, the wind through the rice, Kishmish's hungry bleating. I know what he wants. He wants the leaves from his favourite bush near our house, the one with the tiny red and white flowers. I've forgotten to bring them as I do every morning. I turn and run back.

The bush to the side is almost bare because I've given so many of its leaves to Kishmish. I have to find another bush soon. Then I remember Kurbani Eid. In two days, I won't need to find anymore leaves. Tears come to my eyes and the buzzing grows louder again. I shake my head violently and then carefully bend a leaf stalk where it meets the branch. It comes off easily with a snap, a silky liquid forming a bubble at the base. I wonder what the leaf tastes like. I look around. There's no one close, so I put the leaf in my mouth and chew. The buzzing in my head makes my chewing sound loud, as if someone has plugged up my ears. The leaf breaks into slivers in my mouth and I spit green fibres on the ground. It tastes horrible. But

Kishmish likes it so I get a few more leaves and run back to the paddy, spitting leaf bits on the way.

Abba straightens and looks at me as I stand on the embankment. My uncle is beside him, and Kishmish a few metres away. I wipe my mouth with the back of my hand.

'Are you the one trampling your uncle's field?' Abba asks. His voice is like the river, but different every day. Some days, I am like a boat and can follow it, seeing everything. Other times, I can't even come close because the water is too fast. Today, I am a fish underwater in Abba's river, not understanding what is happening above the water. But I can feel Abba's feelings, water currents against my fish body. I stand on one leg as if it were a fish tail and twist about, trying to listen.

'Of course you're the culprit,' Abba says impatiently, turning away. 'You and that stupid goat. Jah, bhag! Get out!'

Kishmish moves a little and then turns back towards Abba. Abba raises his hand.

'Kishmish, come here!' I shout.

My uncle looks at me, then whispers something to Abba.

Abba replies, 'It's just the way he talks. He'll

outgrow it. I am more concerned with the fact that he doesn't listen.'

'You should consider that madrasa I told you about, the one that just opened up near town. I hear it straightens out wayward boys.'

Abba shrugs and shoos Kishmish towards me. Kishmish runs and leaps out of the paddy to get his leaf. As he snuffles noisily in my palm, the buzzing in my ears dies down.

The night before Eid, I tell Ammu that we have to save Kishmish.

'He's not very big. Maybe we can find another goat for Abba,' I say, pulling at her sari.

'Alo, I'm cooking for tomorrow, can't you see?' Ammu says, straightening her anchal. She presses her lips together, making her lipstick look darker. Abba says Ammu is too proud of her looks, that she's just a weaver's wife and there is no need for airs, for the lipstick she craves. But I like it when she wears lipstick. She makes smacking fish lips at me, and I try not to move as her lips close in, soft and damp, closer and closer, till I can see each red crease separately, velvet that envelopes first my vision and then every other sense. At the last minute, I scream and run away, laughing.

'She's going to cook Kishmish tomorrow!' Joy

crows from the corner of the kitchen where he's sitting and eating a shingara, steam rising from the mashed potato inside.

A line of uncooked shingaras sits beside the stove, their doughy edges pressed closed with the tines of our only fork. Ammu slides one into the pan filled with oil, and its body swells unevenly, fizzing and sizzling in the gold liquid.

'You're going to cook Kishmish tomorrow!' I wail.

'Speak clearly,' Joy says sharply.

I look at him, confused. Ammu splashes the shingara over in the oil with the fork and then ruffles my hair.

'Shona, you must forget about the goat. Your father bought him for Kurbani Eid and we have to sacrifice him for God. Abba told you why, no? The story of Ibrahim? Do you want to hear it again?'

'Yes,' I sob. I know all the animal stories by heart, but I love hearing them. The story of the spider that saved Prophet Muhammad's life, and Yunus who was swallowed by a whale, and Nuho and his ark and all the pairs of animals.

'He can't even say yes properly,' Joy says scornfully.

'I can!' I shout, so my voice won't shake. 'Yes, yes, yes!'

But Joy keeps laughing until Ammu slants her eyes at him dangerously. She fishes the shingara out of the oil and bobs in two more.

'Joy's mother,' a voice breaks into the kitchen. We all turn. It's Abba.

Ammu looks at him questioningly.

'Asho,' he says, his voice a slow rise of waves. His shoulders are hunched under his singlet. My body is like Abba's, long and thin. Not like Joy who is rounder and more like Ammu. I don't mind. I'm going to be a weaver like Abba, and I'm going to have lots of goats and not eat any of them.

'I'm cooking,' Ammu says, pointing towards the oily pan.

'I said come, July.'

Ammu's face tightens in fear. She turns off the stove and leaves the kitchen quickly, the bottoms of her feet scratching against the dirt on the concrete floor. I shut my eyes to see if I can tell what's going to happen. All I see are the flames of the stove fire being swallowed into black. The creak of the tin door spins my head around. I look around for Joy, but he's already left the kitchen.

I don't have to move to hear what Abba

is asking, or Ammu's responses. In our house, everything thuds off the cement, rustles through the thatching, chews into the wood beams.

Sometimes I feel invisible. There was an old rickshawallah who cycled Ammu and me home in the rain. His threadbare lungi slapped against his body as he pumped at the pedals. I tried to pull the plastic sheet over Ammu's legs so she wouldn't get wet, but she didn't seem to notice. If I stand still enough, perhaps the world itself will pass through me like the water through fabric.

'My brother said he saw you coming out of the police inspector's house.' Abba's voice is smooth.

'It's not what you think—' Ammu's voice is shaking. A sharp slap sounds, followed by her cry.

'I know that my wife paints herself into a whore when she goes to town.'

Another slap and then a harder sound, and Ammu cries out again.

'And now this. You go to the house of that man. The man who locked your own brother in jail. Have you no shame at all? Even if not for yourself, for your family?'

'He said, he told me he would help Mintu. He said he could help,' Ammu says in a rush, her words all running together.

I remember the day we went to the inspector's house. It had been raining all afternoon and I didn't want to go, but Ammu said we had to. His house was in town, a long way by rickshaw. He started cleaning his gun, putting each piece on the table with a careful click. When Ammu tried to say something, he raised his hand and she fell silent. When he was finished cleaning, he loaded and cocked his pistol at me. Ammu went away and then, so did he. Only a small cloth and a blackened brush sat on the table. I stood in the quiet room, listening to the rain outside, and I thought about Kishmish until Ammu came back, her face still and drawn.

I can no longer separate Abba's words from the slaps. Ammu cries all night. She is trying to be quiet, but I can hear her. I can't sleep. I have to save Kishmish, and Ammu is not going to be able to help me. Maybe I can lead him away from the paddy, far down the river, so he won't be able to find his way back. I won't be able to play with him, but at least he won't die. Yes, that's what I'll do. Suddenly, I feel Abba shaking me.

'Get up,' he says, 'We're going to the masjid.'

Is it morning already? Did I fall asleep? When did Ammu stop crying? Where is Kishmish? Joy is getting dressed in the darkness. He reaches out and pulls me from the pallet, not ungently. I follow him into the compound. Kishmish is tied to a tree close by. I start towards him but Abba pulls me away and we join a stream of men and boys walking to prayers.

Abba keeps me close to him the whole dawn, his hand tight on my wrist, as if he knows what I'm thinking. I usually like the sound of praying, the chanting of all the different voices, but everything sounds scary this morning.

Abba's grip grows firmer as we walk back over the broken brick path to our compound. He tells Joy to bring Kishmish to the far side of the pond. I haven't dared to pull away yet, but when I understand that Abba means to keep me by him while he kills Kishmish, I start struggling and screaming. My voice sounds shrill and weak, and Abba takes no notice. He gives my hand to Joy and tells him not to let go. I heave at Joy who has to use both hands to hold me. I call for Ammu but she's nowhere to be seen.

It's as if Kishmish doesn't know what's happening, even when his legs are tied up. He lies on the muddy ground quietly and even licks Joy's foot. My voice fades inside my head. It is only at the end that Kishmish struggles, when the blood starts coming. By then, I can't hear him. I can hear the blood though, slipping through the grass, brushing the blades aside, sinking into the wet ground. A dot of red opens like a flower on my kurta, and then another. Kishmish watches us, watches himself pool around us. His eye swivels and swivels and then goes flat.

One week after Eid, on a clear breezy day, Abba and Ammu take me on a rickshaw and then on a bus. The fields get farther and farther apart, and soon there are no fields, only rows of shops. Finally, we arrive outside a bright blue building. Ammu waits outside, her burqa floating like a small black cloud against the blue wall. Abba leads me through a courtyard and into a small room. A man sits at a wooden desk, dressed all in white. Abba hands him an envelope and starts speaking. I can't follow his voice anymore. I am too tired.

The man takes my hand and the three of us walk back into the courtyard. I hear a humming sound and turn. It's coming from one of the rooms of the building. The humming turns into chanting. It makes me think of the banana-leaf flute Abba made me during the last monsoon. If you hold the leaf flute tightly at both ends and blow through the holes, it makes a spiralling sound that swells and shrinks.

Abba and Ammu are standing in the courtyard. Ammu's veil is wrapped around her face. Only her eyes are showing. I remember then my future memory, the one I thought false but which is coming true now. I can't say anything because I used up the words before it was time. They turn and walk away, Ammu's burqa billowing in the wind.

Now Go

We're sitting stiff
x-love between us
lying thickly in the sauce
I rest my fork on the edge of the plate
the silence is heavy but it means nothing
because there is nothing between us, anymore.

You say,

>   You're a fool. I gave you everything I had.
>   There's nothing more. You need to move on.

I'm dancing on the strobe of midnight
a roar in my veins, liquid in my bones
You enter in a rush
all hot skin and long limbs
And I disappear inside my head

You say,

>   No one else will suck your tongue
>   like this.
>   No one else will touch you
>   like this.
>   You are so beautiful.
>   You are so beautiful.

Now we're in the bathroom
white lights and mirrors glitter
I watch myself as I always do
but my eyes are clear tonight
of fear, of love, of want even

your hand, so familiar, circles my throat,
and my eyes close, my head tilts back
your tongue traces the arch of my body
hard hip against my heat
I am amazed at my calm
my face is so still
through your words, through your kisses
this could go on forever
    (would that it would)
this could stop right now
    (would that it would)

You say,
    No one else can compare. No one else will
    come close.
    You will always be the one. My first love.
    My best love.
    Now go.

The inside of the ladies' compartment on the Harbour Line train was a toxic bottle-green. The square swinging handles on the ceiling of the car were made of a rusted, roughened metal from another century, but were still deeply coloured. Everything was deeply coloured. The shalwar kameezes in tender orange, hot lime, reserved aquamarine. The saris, all filigreed and feisty and fabulous. There was nothing pale about India.

Rox thrust her body out of the train, gripping a peeling green bar with one hand like the men in the adjoining cars, and watched Bombay collage pass. A boy in shirtsleeves stood at bat on a dead-end street. His posture reminded her of her childhood friend, Raza, easy and elegant. He swung wildly and quickly pressed his fingertips to his mouth in apology. The rest of the boys doubled up, their tattered pants and bare chests contrasting with the batter's pressed outfit, their teeth sharp and shining. At the next station, a ruined mansion focused out of the landscape, threadbare petticoats hanging off exquisitely carved and crumbling balconies.

She didn't know where she was going, but she knew where she was. And by the time she got there, she'd know that too, though she wouldn't know who he was now. It kept going, this onion peel cycle of knowing and unknowing, understanding more and less, every dive-bomb second. It was how it always was. It's how it always is.

I would like to send you
a photograph of myself
any photograph really
because it's a photograph of you
within me

As her train heaved into Bandra, a man crouching on the platform stared right through her, his dark eyes dull and lifeless, his skin made of the grey-brown dust that shrouded everything in winter. She blinked and he blurred into the background.

Even before the train stopped, the pushing and shoving had begun. She wasn't sure why everyone ran after the trains so. Even if you weren't in the first crush, it seemed as if everyone got onto the train. The shoving just made it harder for people to get off. But she didn't mind forcing herself through the brightly wrapped and writhing bodies, and she liked the view from the doorway. It made it easier to jump onto the platform from the crawling car.

She made her way to the exit, ever aware of her height, head and shoulders above the crowds of women. Even when the female streams merged with the male, she could easily make out the ticket stands ahead. She often saw herself in scenes with subtext: tall woman melting reluctantly, inconsistently, into the flow.

Her favourite Bandra West overpass was one of several high footbridges leading to the station exit. She had whipped out her camera in many places so far, but hadn't yet had the courage to detour the hurrying masses around her here.

The setting sun glanced off the shantytown roofs, and purple hazed the sky. A hush came over her brain, fading the raucous rush-hour sounds into silence, swallowing her outer eye. Her hand moved to her camera, and she slowed, feeling people brush past. At the last minute, she let her breath out, the volume turned up, and she walked on.

I'm writing this letter
while eating a mango
standing by the sink
in a Western world

I don't want to drip
over the red wood floor
onto my tight blue jeans
into your eastern hands

You are more beautiful than ever
I am as wanting

She sat beside him in the night, slow dust settling over the city. Her last evening in Bombay would also be their only meeting, their first meeting, after so many years. Mosquitoes were biting her even in this upscale Bandra lounge, and she stamped her sandalled feet, arched her painted toes, hoping he wouldn't notice. He would look down on her if he noticed her fidgeting. Think her more frail than he already did. She had never felt so female before she met Arul, so coy. The finickiness had been taunted out of her many lovers before him. Even India, with its soil and swarth and staring, didn't faze her. But when she was with him, all the things that women were, all the sentimental sensitivities, they rose in her body, oozed through her skin. She sweated girl from every pore, and she hated it. One of these days, she would learn that her feelings, whether brash or butterfly, lived for many reasons, none of which should embarrass her.

I went to India (you) to have sex
of course, once I got there (you)
I couldn't go through with it
it sounds poetic and stupid
but it was the air that did me in

             the pollution burying
           its viscous and viral heart
                    in my lungs

       Albeit my teenage boy libido
                hasn't taken an eye
                      off your fly
                 this entire time

             That's why I can't talk
                       about love
             That's why I can't talk
                   about anything
                         at all

He sat beside her in the night, sprawling in
the wicker chair in crumpled clothes, voice like a
damp garden. She could smell herself through her
silky blue lehenga, through her cotton underwear,
through his disregard. He was interested in
something else, in what went wrong with them
years ago, when they loved and lost each other
in the West. He forked his tandoori chicken with
gusto, and in between bites, he spiked her anger
with his questions. She held onto the feeling,
fingers frozen in mid twirl of her hair, so that she
didn't do the only thing she really wanted to do,
which was kiss him. Instead, she took so long to
reply that it was too late when she found the words.

With *One*, I didn't know
what I wanted
With *Three*, it took me till *Six*
to figure it out
With *Thirteen*, I realized
within days of our demise
One of these days, I'll speak
and you will actually be there

It was late and the dogs had come out onto the streets. They slunk around, jutting their hips so. Intermittent headlights flared their passive eyes into fire. She could see their narrow forms from the terrace, through the bougainvillea vines and sculpted concrete. The city tasted dry on her lips, salty, smoky, old before it was born.

It's not that I don't listen
I always do
I even believe everything you say
despite what you think
I only pretend to mock
because I don't want to seem gullible, too encouraging
of your ways

But even my pretense
is easily punctured
all you'd have to do is look
and you'd know

but you haven't looked at me once
you stopped looking
after the first time we met
It was as if you already knew
what I looked like
and you've never needed
to double-check anything
certainly not something
as simple as my feeling
for you

She had always prided herself on being fast. On saying before thinking. She thought it meant the truth, if it came out without hesitation. But she was drunk on fresh lime soda and vodka by the time she was ready to talk, and being drunk made her slow, more reluctant to play by her hard and fast rules.

'How is it, then, Roxanne,' he asked, gesturing widely, 'being here?'

She watched his hand move in slow motion as she replied, 'Stranger, and more familiar than I expected.'

'I knew you would like it,' he said, relaxing, turning back to his plate.

'I knew you would say that,' she said, turning away.

'It's not like that,' he said. 'I just meant you would understand.'

You have never known
how to look outside yourself
You have always assumed
that you know better
You have never understood
that there are multiple ways to understand the world
and so many more multiple ways
to be

The waiters huddled in the corner of the terrace, outnumbering the guests three to one. It was the same everywhere, this luxury of staff. It was easy to get used to the fawning service. She could even forget their eyes following her every motion, until her eyes met theirs and they started away. It was the ones outside that she couldn't forget, the ones who weren't watching. Bombay was a stranger to itself. More than half its inhabitants in slums, perched on the edges of rail lines, crammed under bridges, crowding into the polluted horizon. She knew she was unused to the poverty, and more than that, she was aghast at the scale of it. But none of this was new. It was the oldest fact of life, despair.

He said she was looking at it all wrong. The grey, peeling buildings weren't grim or dreary. They were a reminder of the rains. The sprawling slums weren't shocking. They were another place to live.

Look, he told her, they even have electric lines feeding through the narrow alleyways, powering the occasional TV and refrigerator.

It wasn't despair. It was just life.

> I have never known
> how to stay inside myself
> I have always assumed
> it was better after it was over
> I have never understood
> that being righteous
> is another path to illumination
> one more way to honour
> the singular force of life
> the singular life
> of feeling

She stood up, and a waiter lurched towards them.

'Can we go inside? The mosquitoes are biting me,' she said, her voice sharp. She shook her head at the waiter and he retreated. 'And don't tell me I'm weak because of it, because I *am* weak because of it.'

'Don't be strident,' he said as they walked towards the cold white sofas inside the lounge.

The air conditioner prickled her skin. He stretched beside her, depressing the sticky vinyl between them, forcing her leg against his. The sugar on her tongue crystallized, and she fell silent, looking to the dance floor below with its swirling lights and gyrating bodies. She wasn't speaking to him because he said she was being strident. She wasn't speaking to him because he was right.

'You're upset, aren't you?' he asked after a moment. 'Because I shouldn't have said what I said.'

And in taking the blame, he instantly made her see that it was hers.

You told me you were stoic
but I don't think you know
what stoic really means
it's my one talent that
I'm still a little bit in love
with everyone I've ever loved

You, on the other hand,
you forget everything, everything
except for what remains
in your line of sight

                    under your hands
                    but your hands
            you have the most beautiful hands

        I forgive you everything, everything
                    when you touch me
            everything except for my need

'Let's dance,' he said, draining his beer and holding out his hand. 'I never danced with you when we were together. You always felt bad about that.'

She started to argue until she realized that what he meant was that *he* had always felt bad about it. The rainbow disco lights stabbed at them, edging them as she curved her arms around him. She felt like she was falling through the spiralling lights. Or maybe she was falling for him again, the way you fall in love with someone you see after a long time. But it was happening at the end of her holiday, on their only night together.

So why didn't it work between them? When did she start becoming disappointed? Where did he go wrong? How did she sleep with Sailan so soon afterwards? He was asking the easiest questions in the world. She'd told everyone else the answers. She'd even told him. But, for some reason, as soon as he asked, it became a mystery again, and she felt forced to say something different. Not that she knew what. Not that she knew why they were talking about them, when it was over years ago, half a world away.

> Nothing went wrong between us (anyone)
> Nothing at all
> It (everyone) was always meant to be
> even as it would have never worked out
> And aren't we all disappointed
> in the end?

'Let's go,' she said, pulling away from him, unable to stay in the moment. She was longing for her stale sepia bedsheets, the hot still room in which she had been sleeping the last few days. Her colleague's spare elegant apartment was silent all its hours, except for the faint infrequent rumble of the trains to the west. She liked it that way, and not just for the easy metaphor of refuge from the madness of Bombay. In its unfamiliar and encompassing smell, sound and sight, it was a refuge from anything she could conjure up at all.

'I'll take you to yours,' he said, as they emerged from the artificially cooled air of the club into the warm dusty night. The streets were deserted now. A lone black taxi was parked at the phone booth, its driver draped over the steering wheel. They started walking down Linking Road with its fancy shops dark and gated. Her palm felt sweaty in his and she shifted her arm uncomfortably only to find his grip tightening.

I push and I pull
I watch and I wait
I tire of being the one who wants

I don't have the courage
to speak up and take it
I don't have the wisdom
to know it's not mine

but I know this much
what's over isn't a failure
what's perfect isn't forever

I'm in love with the memory of us
And I don't ever have to fall
out of that

Outside the building where she was staying, she asked, 'Will you come up?'

'I will, for a little while,' he said. 'Even though the doorman will know, tell all the neighbours, and ruin your colleague's reputation.'

'Are you serious? He's not even here.'

'He's of marriageable age, isn't he? You're lucky his mother doesn't live here too. She would have a fit.' He switched from his deep, modulated colonial-educated voice to a dramatic Indian accent. 'You're sullying his chances of finding a suitable bride.'

She laughed even as she wrapped her glittering dupatta more carefully around her body. But as soon as she stepped through the gate, the night watchman perked up from his seemingly unconscious state and watched them through puffy slits of eyes. He glanced at his watch as they walked past him to the elevator. She pursed her lips. He was right, as usual.

It must be hard for you
all these womengirls
making their tragic mistakes
around you
with other men
against everyone's better judgement

If only they could see what you see
it would be so much easier
if they understood their flaws
managed their uncertainties
overcame their weaknesses

recognized their powers
said what they thought
took what they wanted

Or maybe the men like you
can't imagine for a moment
that the place where women live
is alien ground
or that sometimes
we can only believe what we hear
or perhaps most remarkably
that judgement isn't the only response

She switched on the fan as they entered the room, and sprawled on the bed. The giant mirror in the front of the room reflected her prostrate form in the darkness, his pacing one.

'Sit,' she said, wanting him to lie down or leave. He drew open the curtains and looked outside. The light of the moon filled the room.

'You haven't answered my questions,' he said, looking out at the silhouetted trees.

She sat up and unwound the dupatta from her body. 'It's because I'm not sure why you're asking.'

'I'm asking because when do you get a chance to talk about these things with the very person, to understand what happened?' He sat down beside her.

She said nothing, unhooking the back of her kameez, pulling it over her head, loosening her hair. He caught a few strands and wound them into a knot around his hand, a familiar gesture. In the mirror, she watched his fist settle between her naked shoulder blades, his fingers shadowy against her skin. She leaned towards him but he let go and walked back to the window. She sighed and turned her back to him, lying down on the hard bed.

> Look again
> I found you
> the you I dreamed
> that other night
> this other life
> under moonlight
> my hair coiled into your palm

Was it the moonlight on her skin that made him surrender? Or her silence that pushed him into a physical space? She didn't know, but in moments, she felt his hand pushing up her lehenga, quickly, expertly, feeling, finding, filling her softness. But he came too quickly, his mouth pressed into her pulsing throat. He didn't wait for her even though she was so close, so close.

> It's true I'm not lost
> I know where I stand
> I'm only waiting
> for lightning to strike
>
> look again
> I am more beautiful than ever
> You are as full
> and the lightning
> is only waiting
> for me

The ceiling fan sliced easily, slowly, through the warm air. He stood up, pulling on his jeans, restless, eager to move. In the distance, a Harbour Line train clanked indistinctly into the station. She had a sudden desire to be on the train again, alone with strangers and the wind.

'Have a good night,' he said, startling her with his voice. He was standing at the door, jiggling his feet.

She shook her head. What a send off, those words. 'Sure,' she said as she stretched back towards the moon and closed her eyes. 'You too.'

He stilled. 'What I meant to say was, thank you,' he said. 'It was beautiful to see you, and touch you again. I will dream of your skin tonight.'

She nodded, and then smiled. 'I know.'

I have stolen everything
in this glitty world
knowledge, perspective, vision

All of it
I've borrowed and bought
sorrowed and sought

Even these words
their very order
none of it is original

I claim only
your immediate pleasure
as my own

AFTER THE LOVE

Mahalingapuram, Chetput, Egmore, Chennai
  Central
6 little girls your age
Gudur, Nellore, Vijawada, Eluru
5 about your height
Rajamundry, Samalkot, Duvvada, Vishakapatnam
4 skipping instead of walking
Berhampur, Khurda Road, Bhadrak, Kharagpur
3 with eyes as bright
Kolkata, Howrah Junction, Marquis Street,
  Haridaspur
2 tossing hair so fine
Benapol, Jessore, Dhaka, Kamalapur Bus Station
1 with feet too small
Shantinagar, Tejgaon, Gulshan
after all the love
Gulshan Avenue, Road 103, Wonderland
there are endless ways to fall

When I was young, I had nightmares about marrying a silent man like my father. In the beginning of the dream, he would start off garrulous, and then gradually the weight of the world would swallow up his words, one by one. I would ask him increasingly louder questions, hoping my volume would turn his up. Instead, I would end up shouting into his silence. Sometimes my shout would reach across from the dreaming place into the waking place, a diminished sound that yet roused you, my sister. You slept beside me on a prickly pati in our one-room shack, and despite not being fully awake, you would pull me close to yourself, reminding me where we both were.

'Asho, Komola,' you would murmur into my hair, smoothing it with your hand, 'I'm here.'

My hair was my only asset that equalled yours. It grew glossily, copiously from my scalp. Everything else, though, marked you for more. You were fairer, taller, sweeter. We knew you would marry well.

My father was a rickshawallah. He sometimes made enough money for two meals a day, but not enough for two dowries. Each night, he would park his rickshaw with the others, in pairs facing one another in lockstep, and return exhausted, his gaunt face made even more pitiable by his expression. The other fathers never looked as tired or thin. What was it about my father's lot that had aged him so? I didn't know, and it made me angry. He made me angry. Did he have to suffer so outwardly? It only made things worse for the rest of us. As soon as he entered our home, we had to stop playing with our baby brother, Mintu, and stand about looking as sad as he. You could sometimes make him smile. You would silently act out the day's adventures in clownish detail and if you caught him at the right time during his smoke, something would lift and the evening wouldn't be as oppressive.

I was twelve when I left home. My first menses cycle ended with a pregnancy, but I lost my husband and then my baby in quick succession. Everything in the village reminded me of everything I didn't want to think about. So I went to Dhaka where nothing looked familiar.

A few months later, you were married off to a weaver and were soon heavy with child. If I had been at home, I would have tried to persuade our father not to send you away. To wait even just one more year, and surely you would find someone better. I know you at least would have listened to me. You always did, even though I was younger. There was something about you that was childlike. It made me afraid for you. I was the one who held your hand jumping across the ditch leading to our home, the one who chased away the boys desiring your attention. But by then

I was far away in Dhaka, working as a maid in a lavish flat filled with glass and knickknacks, a far cry from the sparse and wood of my childhood.

Much later, you showed up at my employer's doorstep, more beautiful with the years. I couldn't talk to you very long because the master of the house was very strict and would beat me for any wrongdoing, sometimes for nothing I could understand.

I shuffled nervously at the front door and asked, 'July, what happened? What are you doing here?'

'I have left everything. My husband, our village, my sons, Joy, my sweet boy Alo. Oh, my Alo,' you said, your voice breaking on the name. 'I'm working in a garment factory outside Dhaka.'

'Why did you leave? Where are you living?'

'I'm in Gazipur, with Mintu. He escaped from the jail, and ran away with me. But he wants me to quit because the overseers at the factory are always harassing me. I won't. At the factory, they pay us more than Abba made as a rickshawallah, and my money is all mine. I don't have to give it to anyone.'

'Listen, I cannot talk long,' I told you, taking your soft hands into my calloused ones. I did not know that this would be the last time I would see you.

'Come with me,' you said to me. I could hear the earnestness, the desperation. 'Forget working as a maid. We can live together and work at the same factory.'

'You must go,' I said, not considering your offer for a second. At the time, I was so consumed by fear of my employer, it was impossible for me to think of anything else. The elevator door opened, making me start. But it was only a peon going to the opposite flat. You left then, after touching my hair the way you used to. I shut the door and went back to work.

I heard nothing from you for so long that I got worried. I used what free afternoons I had to look for you. I finally found Mintu in Chittagong, near our old village home. He told me that you had not come home for several months. He said he had searched everywhere, hearing all the while rumours about pretty garment workers being sold at high prices, to work as sex slaves in India. He was drunk and told me this in a surly manner, his voice dry, as if it meant nothing to him. I could not shake the feeling that he was somehow responsible for your disappearance, but there was nothing I could do. That night, I did not return to my employer's flat. Nor the next night, nor the night after. Eventually, I found another place to work, a house where if you returned, you might be able to stay with me.

But this is all history. Unforgotten, but so many years ago, it no longer moved me. Until now. Until you. My love, my husband, I am beginning to understand how dreams come true. When I married the first time, I was barely out of girlhood and had no real conception of what it meant to love. When my first husband died, and then God called my baby daughter only months later, I thought my time for love had run out. But years later, Tahsin was born, the younger son of my new employers, and I felt another lease beginning, a contraction inside my chest so that it seemed all the space inside me was taken up when I held his tiny plump body to mine. In no time at all, it felt as if my heart had always been this full.

When Tahsin left for America seventeen years later, I cried harder than his mother. I had reason to. It was I who had raised him, after all. I knew when best to wake him in the mornings before school, how much rice to put on his plate, what each of his gestures and expressions meant. Some mornings, I wake and find myself standing in his old room. I look around, my thick braid slapping against my back bringing me into the present, and the neatly made bed only confuses me further. Then I remember that he's gone.

It was not long after Tahsin left that I met you, my husband, my bane, with your quick smile, your quicker hands. I thought God had blessed me yet again. All the beatings, the barren hours, it all faded under your gaze. I was so proud when people saw us together, when they saw you, your hair shining and combed, your clothes carefully pressed no matter how well worn, and most of all, your eyes, so large, so lashed. Looking at you made my heart happy. It still would now, despite my anger.

You haven't come to see me in ten months. Perhaps it's a blessing. Perhaps, if you came, I'd throw my pride to the wind and forget myself. I'd believe your protests of love and preoccupation, once again. I might even give you more money, even though I've promised myself no more. It's just that, when I hear your plans, your filmi-deep voice, so excited for a future that I imagine includes me, I want nothing more than to make it work. For you. For us. But it seems that you've deliberately forgotten me, your beloved wife in the city.

I had to cancel my trip to my village this winter because of you. For weeks, you didn't take my calls. I'd hear ring after hollow ring in my tin ear, the one that hasn't worked well since my accident at the well. With each successive call, the number of rings would get shorter, until finally, you just shut off your phone and I gave up, the space between my reaching out and your rejection too small to bear. Then, finally, one day, you called up and as soon as I answered, I felt my heart treacherously open. Still, I had to ask, though I was so afraid it would push you away from me.

'Where have you been?' I asked as evenly as possible. 'I have been calling for so long.'

'I have been so busy, my dearest. Someone I once called a friend was minding my store while I went to Chittagong. When I got back, I found he had cheated me by starting his own mobile shop and stealing my best suppliers. I have spent the last few months trying to find another supplier. It has been very difficult…' Your voice trailed off, hurriedness mingling with quiet.

'You went to Chittagong? Was it to see my brother?'

'I didn't want to tell you because I knew you might be angry.'

'Why would I be angry?' I asked, though I could already feel myself becoming so.

'You know why.'

'You should not be talking to him. I know he is our brother, but I am sure he sold July, or had something to do with it. I wish you had never met him.'

'Mintu can help me. Help us. Maybe even help your sister. But he is always drunk and he doesn't speak to everyone. So I had to use other means.'

I know what you did. You have power in those beguiling eyes of yours. You recite from the hadiths, backwards, and the unintelligible staccato words make men thrill with fear and women do what you want. Is that how you got me? Did you mumble a prayer in reverse under your breath when we met? Did I fall because of your secret art or the darker art of love?

God may strike me down for saying this, but does it matter? I cannot breathe either way. I hurt. I wish I had been able to go to school because I know that learned people hurt less.

Rich people, even lesser. I am not educated or rich, so I don't know how to escape the pain, nor can I buy my way out of it. I know nothing except for how to cook, how to clean, how to love all the wrong people. July. Then Tahsin. Now you. Only my sister did not betray my love. But she is gone.

'I want to go to my village,' I told you, feeling a keen desire for my childhood home. 'But I could not go. I cannot return without you. How would it look?'

'I cannot go now.'

'Then visit me more often in Dhaka.'

'I cannot,' you said evenly.

'Are you angry with me?' I asked you. 'Because if you are, I will die. I will.' And I felt the truth of the statement, his disdain filling me, pushing the air out of my body, leaving me hollow.

'I am not angry,' you said. 'We will go to your village next month. After Eid. If your brother helps me, all will be well. You can have your wedding feast as you wished so long ago. I just need enough cash for next month and then the profits will start coming in. We will be throwing money around.'

This cold marble floor that I clean every day,

this is where my life begins, this is where it ends. I see now I made a mistake. But I'm going to fix it. I'm going to make you do what you must. I know how I'll do it too. I'll lure you with the promise of the money you need. You haven't paid your shop rent in weeks. Your oldest son needs to pay his tuition fees. The youngest needs new shoes. So when I tell you I want to draw up the papers to share my property, my money, you'll jump at the chance.

I never asked you for much. I didn't care if you never returned the one lakh taka you borrowed from me three years ago to start your shop. Money I had saved from years of breaking my back for people who would beat me for one shattered glass animal, one wrong word.

I didn't ask you to leave your wife and children in Mymensingh. I didn't need jewellery or a pretty sari. All I wanted was time. A visit a few times a year. Some days here. A week there. Perhaps twenty altogether. Isn't that only fair, a score for love?

Weeks passed before I was able to put my plan into action. I had to find someone I trusted to write the contracts. The darwan gave me his name and the name of a man who would act as security. I met them both separately and spoke at length about my plan.

Finally, the day came. You arrived late. We had been sitting in a tiny airless office for almost two hours. The security man had relaxed his upright stance long ago, and was slouched against the wall. Three mismatched cups and saucers sat in front of us on the old wooden table, filled and refilled, and refilled once again with watery tea.

I had not seen you in more than a year. You looked the same beautiful same, while I felt I had aged terribly. When I took your hand and held it, you looked at me strangely. You couldn't know, could you, how I was going to keep you close?

Two pieces of paper lay on the table. The first one, the one whose colour and the shape of the writing I had memorized, listed all my assets, money, my father's thatched shack in the village, along with a small corner of land. When the contract man had first showed me the ivory coloured sheet with its typed ink depressions, I felt bereft. Could someone's life, her worth, fit onto one side of a sheet of paper? In between the words, words I couldn't read myself, was space. There was space above the words, and below. It looked wanting. Where were the decades I had

spent in my current employer's house, the years
in the glass-filled flat before that? Where marked
the day Tahsin was born, the night I met you,
the last afternoon I saw my sister? What about
the dozen years I shared with my family in my
village? You wouldn't know from this thin sheet
how my body travailed during the day, how my
heart folded at night.

This paper, the rolls of taka, the piece of land,
these were the only physical things I had. Perhaps
it was better this way, to focus on these. The
intangible things, the ones that made you feel, I
was better off without them.

The other contract, a blinding white sheet of
paper, had even more empty space on it. As I had
instructed the contract man, it stated that you
had borrowed one lakh taka from me three years
ago with the intention of paying it back within
ten years. We had seven years left though I had
no intention of making you pay me back. I only
wanted a way to hold on to you. A way to bring
you back if you lost me.

You shook my hand loose and started reading
the contracts. It took you longer than I expected,
but I waited.

You picked up the second paper, the one

outlining your debt to me, and asked, 'What is this for?'

I said nothing, embarrassed at my need. Now that you were standing there, so solid, so real, the precaution seemed unnecessary. Like a tattered white flag of my dignity.

'You want me to sign this?'

I nodded and then shrugged.

'And this other document?'

Your tone was distant, giving my shame room to lie down, spread out.

I gathered breath and said, 'It means everything I have is yours. If you sign this one, you must sign the other one too.'

'And then what?'

'And then nothing. It's only to show you what I have, what I want.'

'We know what we have, my dear,' you said. 'We don't need these papers to tell us that. But if this is what you want to do, so be it.'

You bent and signed both papers with a flourish. I added my thumb signature on the line the contract man pointed to, and then carefully folded the papers and put them into my purse. Madam had given me this purse years ago, an old aubergine-coloured leather purse she was going to throw away because the inner cloth pockets had torn. The contracts fit perfectly under the silver clasp.

As I tucked the purse under my arm, I caught you exchanging a look with the contract man. Did it mean anything? I don't know. What I do know is that you didn't stay the weekend as you promised. You stayed one night, and the next morning you were gone, as was my aubergine purse containing the contracts and the new red lipstick I had bought at a terribly expensive store in Gulshan, for the occasion of seeing you.

I wish you would have stayed longer. I could have given you the money I had saved out of my month's salary, kept the lipstick. Instead, I cried all day and into the evening.

At night, Madam opened the door to my room. I thought she was going to scold me for neglecting my work. Instead, she told me there was someone here to see me, a family relation of mine. I knew no one who would come visit me, but I wiped my face and went downstairs.

I opened the heavy wooden door, and it was you, my sister, standing straight, looking older, yet younger. I never thought I would see you again. You must have gone so far, but then returned. The space in my body contracted to an endless point.

'July,' I said, starting crying all over again. This time beloved. This time in fullness.

THE ALPHABET GAME

A... B... C...
the tree was throwing shadows
monsters and aliens
invading his room

a stray branch hit the roof
again and again
he was using it for rhythm
he was using it for time

D... Clack. E... Clack.
F... Clack.
he had no idea
what he was doing

Three months ago, Raza's life turned inside out. Three months ago, his older sister, Juthi, came back from the bad girls' school to start her junior year. The house he had begun to think of as his own had become overrun by girls. Juthi's girlfriends were very different from the girls he knew in eighth grade. They laughed when he least expected, pouted through their fears, screamed when they got their way. The girls he was used to were less strident, less effusive, far less threatening.

Juthi had always mystified him. She had never paid much attention to their broken family, least of all to him. But her time away had imbued her with a manic extroversion, which extended sloppily, inconsistently, into his life. She could spend an hour asking him animated questions about middle school, or leafing through his comic books, and then ignore him for days. He wondered sometimes whether she was still on drugs, and if they were the right kind or the wrong kind. Either way, he wasn't sure if he really wanted to know.

Juthi and Raza didn't look or act alike. This much hadn't changed. She took after their mother, dark skin and eyes, while Raza had more of their Italian American father's features, honey-hazel all over. And while he had always been the quieter one in the family, now he felt almost invisible beside her, with her rushed and rough ways.

Her friends treated him with indifference or sophomoric sexuality, very little in between. He found himself both resenting and eager for their visits, their chaotic swarming into the house, raiding the cupboards, pushing him from the sofa, pulling him to the table, leaving behind a cooling charge, the house as silent and stiff as his body.

Today, he returned from school to an empty house. It was Friday and his mother would be home late after teaching a night class at the community college. He peered into the kitchen as he stamped his icy boots on the doormat. The kitchen counter was littered with crumpled aluminum sheets and half-empty take-out containers. Juthi and her friends had been home already. He poured himself a cup of cold coffee from the pot and sipped it while gathering the foil. The containers were from an Indian restaurant. Ever since the divorce, his mother had had little interest in cooking. He looked at the overflowing trash in distaste and then left the foil on the counter, before heading upstairs.

Thankfully, he had not been asked to move out of Juthi's old room when she returned. That would have been too much to bear. He had set it up a far cry from how Juthi had had it. He had got rid of everything except for the bed and desk. The walls had been stripped of the posters, and even the curtains were gone. He liked the sparseness of it, and even the draftiness seemed to fit. He wasn't allowed to turn on the heater during the day, but if he left his coat on, it wasn't so bad.

The walk-in closet, which he had converted into a studio, was a different story. The walls here were plastered with ink sketches, some of comic-book characters, but mostly of creatures he made up in his head. The little room was always comfortably warm, and even had a good-sized window. Good for art, even in winter. You could climb out on the ledge from the window, although he never did when his mother was around. Juthi had used the ledge as her smoking spot, and fallen off not long after transitioning from marijuana to meth.

The window was above the roof of the backyard patio, which was surrounded by hydrangea. The husk of an old apple tree rose from the bushes, a few sturdy branches propped up on the roof, as if it were trying to peer into the closet. When Juthi rolled off the roof, she had reached for the apple tree and missed. Pitching headlong into the bushes, she had broken an arm, and depleted the last of their parents' patience. United for once, they had sent her off to a school in New Mexico that their father had heard about from a friend. A week after she left, Raza had jumped off the roof onto a branch of the apple tree, and then swung down over the bushes to the ground. Just to see what it was like. It wasn't easy, but it wasn't that hard either.

G... Clack. H... Clack.

The perpetual hoarseness of her voice was audible even in her breath, an unevenness as she inhaled, but then the sound drowned with his tongue and the wet.

As he looked through his latest sketchbook in his art room, a sound came from the backyard. The yard was still, and air curled out of the frosted edges of the open window. Then he saw the branches of the elm tree by the back fence quiver. They were in his old tree house, and they had just spied him watching.

'Raza!'

He knew that yodeling voice. It was Lin Yao, a friend of Juthi's whom he liked the least because the small amount of attention she paid him was usually cruel.

'Come down here!' she called.

He shook his head and swallowed the last of his coffee. Lin Yao stuck her head out of the tree, her long black hair falling like liquid over her face. He could see the pink of her cheeks from the house.

'Come on!' she shouted again. 'We need to ask you something. It's a biology thing and you're good at science, Juthi says.'

He went downstairs reluctantly, put his cup in the kitchen sink, and walked out the back door. The snow crunched under his boots, and he could smell cigarette smoke in the still air. Snowflakes were starting to fall again. When he got to the foot of the tree, he stopped and looked up.

After a moment, Lin Yao's head appeared at the trap door opening. 'Oh, you're here. Why didn't you say anything?'

He shrugged, shoving his hands into his pockets.

'Climb up here!' Lin Yao said, her breath hanging like an exclamation.

Raza briefly berated himself for his inability to resist her orders, and started climbing up. As soon as he got to the trap door, he was lifted bodily by four pairs of hands into the house, and forced against the wood plank floor. One arm was held painfully twisted behind his back, and taut smooth girl bodies pinned his legs. Lin Yao straddled his torso, curtaining his view with her silk hair.

'Juthi!' he called before Lin Yao's cold hand

covered his mouth, not that he knew whether Juthi was masterminding the whole thing. He tasted tar on his lips.

'She's not here,' Lin Yao mumbled, her cigarette wobbling in the corner of her mouth. 'She's in detention. Your mom is going to be PO'ed. Doesn't she have a zero tolerance policy?'

She didn't wait for an answer and turned around so her narrow back was to his face. Raza closed his eyes and concentrated on the pain of his twisted arm to distract himself from his reluctant but rising arousal. It was dark in the tree house, and the red tips of their cigarettes flashed like fireflies. He felt Lin Yao's hands on his zipper, and he jerked.

'We just want to see,' she said, twisting around. She stubbed her cigarette out on the greying wood and he resisted the temptation to see if it left a mark. 'Darlene had a theory that you were bigger than my boyfriend.'

Darlene's voice sounded from somewhere near his feet, 'I didn't say that! We should let him go.'

'What? So you can check for yourself? I don't think so.' Lin Yao started to unzip his pants. He couldn't see who the other girls were, but heard one of them giggle.

Juthi's voice floated up towards them, 'Lin?'

Raza was immediately released, but eight hands hovered close. He felt the warmth slowly ebb from his body with a combination of relief and regret. Lin Yao looked out of the tree house.

'Oh, you're back from detention already?' she said casually. 'We were just waiting for you up here. We'll come down.' She turned to Raza and hissed, 'Stay here until we're gone, okay?'

He rubbed his arm as they jostled and clambered over him. Darlene left last. She bent down towards him, her toffee skin and wiry black hair filling his senses.

'Sorry,' she whispered in her half-broken voice. She touched his thigh with an electric motion, and disappeared down the ladder, leaving him instantly hard again.

When Raza finally climbed down, the wind had picked up and it was snowing harder. Lin Yao and the other girls seemed to have left, and Juthi was talking energetically to Darlene in the darkening kitchen about how she had talked her way out of detention. They didn't see him, but he ducked anyway as he crept up the stairs. He couldn't lock his warped bedroom door, but he could lock his art room, so he dragged his sleeping bag into the closet and sat down against the door.

I… Clack. J… Clack. K… Clack.

Her thighs tightened around his head. Maybe it actually worked, this alphabet game. He had heard about it in the gym locker room last year. But the pressure of her limbs was rushing the blood to his face. He felt dizzy and hot, and the shadows of the imaginary creatures were distracting him even as her smell and feel overwhelmed everything else.

He woke suddenly. It was dark, and the porch light was pouring in through the closet window. A knock sounded softly on his door and he realized what had woken him up.

'Raza,' came a whisper, 'it's me, Darlene. Let me in.'

He said nothing.

'I'm alone, I swear. I just want to talk. I can't sleep…'

He shifted silently on the floor. Moments later, he heard footsteps walking away. When the person sounded sufficiently far away, he unlocked the door and opened it slowly. A slice of light connected the closet to the bedroom door. Darlene stood at the far end of the slice, wearing a long t-shirt and Juthi's old pink fluffy slippers.

She smiled. 'I knew you were in there. Can I come in?'

He hesitated and then nodded, pulling the door open wider, getting up from the floor.

'This is your art room, isn't it?' she said, her voice cracked and gentle. He nodded. The closet was too small for two people to stand next to each other without touching. He pushed his clothes closer together to make more room, stumbling over a pile of sketchbooks in the process.

'Show me your drawings,' she said, ignoring his fumble, leaning against the window. 'Juthi says you're really good.'

He hesitated, surprised at this revelation.

'Any one. Maybe in this book.'

'Those aren't finished,' he said quickly.

'Okay, another one then,' she said. He picked up a worn sketchbook and thumbed through it, and then looked up at her. She pulled down the top of the book, watching him, the light from the back porch silhouetting her frame.

'Okay, this one,' he said, flipping the book

around towards her. The jagged lines of the drawing receded under her bent head.

She examined it for a long time before responding, 'It's flying away.' She glanced up at him. 'It's a bird?'

'Close,' he answered. 'It's not anything real. But it is escaping somewhere.'

L… Clack. M… Clack.

She moaned, and so he tongued N more slowly and widely, his mouth reaching the wings of her inner thighs. In this light, his hands looked like white handprints against her skin. He was starting to like this game. He could almost tell when he would make her gasp. The knocking of the branch was just incidental percussion now.

He shut the sketchbook and leaned towards her, and then jerked away awkwardly. She looked at him curiously.

He gestured to the window. 'It's hot. I was going to open…'

'Oh. Go ahead,' she said, moving away from the sill towards him. He reached around her and tugged the window open wider. Her coal hair spiralled over his shoulder and he realized he was still wearing his jacket. Cold air slid in, intensifying the smell of cigarettes and candy on her breath. He shrugged his jacket off, dropping it on the floor beside the sleeping bag.

She touched his t-shirt. 'This too,' she said, helping him pull it off. He felt self-conscious about his thinness, but tried not to hunch. The apple tree knocked against the roof. She started at the sound and he laughed. He had heard the branch bang so many times, it barely registered anymore. She pressed her hand against his mouth to silence him, and started to unzip his pants. The memory of Lin Yao and this afternoon struck him. But Darlene's hands smelled like soap, not ashes, and her hair moved much slower than silk.

S. And S, again, tracing the letter in reverse. Her hips moved in time with an undetermined beat.

V, and a quickening. Her hand grasped his almost painfully. The porch light coming through the window, the sleeping bag sliding under his knees, the undulating winter air above them, all forgotten.

'Darlene? Are you in here?'
Juthi was in Raza's bedroom, her footsteps

echoing as she approached the closet. He raised his head to look at Darlene, his eyes and skin shining. Then he lowered his face to her thighs, kissed her, and grabbed his clothes, jumping out the window. Darlene stood, her t-shirt falling to cover her as the door started to open.

As Raza swung off the apple tree into the thin air, he heard Darlene's voice, 'I couldn't sleep… I thought I'd check out your brother's art, but he's not here…'

He landed in the snow, naked, clutching his clothes to his chest, and then ran, crouched and trembling, out of the light.

THE HUNGRY YEARS

follow the eastern sun
into the eastern sky
climb the shrugging shoulders
of the Mediterranean tide

be the weltering wind
skip slip slide
catch the crumbling wave
run the crushing ride

brown skin
blue bruise
red blood line

get off the ground
ignore the seep
follow the sun
back into the deep

I t wasn't Gabriel's looks that gave him the nerve. Perhaps the years would chisel his baby face into his brother's high cheek-boned grace, but for now he looked much younger than his fifteen years. He was shorter than most of the other boys in his class, his body all bone and scrawny muscle. And, of course, he was darker, darker than even the rest of his family, leading to comparisons with North Africans and other undesirables.

What Gabriel did have on his side was a sharp sly tongue, which he used to cut back at any bullies. Once, their language teacher had paused to let him finish an insult, and used the same metaphor to make his next grammatical point. He grew his midnight hair rockstar long. But most of all, it was the hunger he exuded that was hard to resist. Not just his, but the desire he imagined everyone else had. For each other. For him. Gabriel had learned this lesson early, that wanting begat wanting. The only problem was once the love was his, how was he to leave?

'You're mine,' Carme said, her breath hot on his ear, her fingers hooked possessively into his belt. 'No one else can have you.'

Carme and Gabriel were standing in the middle of a narrow street in Barceloneta. Multicoloured streamers and clotheslines whipped above their heads. A sliver of the Mediterranean gleamed blue in the distance, too far away to see the white-tipped waves, much less the wind surfers. As always, a faint smell of urine lingered in the air. Nearby, two hawkers stood outside a bar under a date palm, smoking hash and arguing about a pair of Nike shoes lost in a recent run from the police. Gabriel thought he caught words in Tamil, but the gist was lost in the wind.

Carme, sensing his distraction, pulled him against her tensile body. She was straddling her bike and the fork banged painfully against his shin. Their shadows cast a miniature version of their drama on the asphalt.

Gabriel shook his hair loose, his hand automatically moving down her back, under her long brown plait, his fingers searching for bare skin. Carme's blouse was closely fit, the pleats of her skirt freshly ironed, as per Señora Casals's highly evolved sense of propriety and fashion. His hand paused as he remembered her mother. Señora Casals was imposingly beautiful and a terror to all the boys Carme brought home. Since Carme fluctuated between bare tolerance and outright hatred of her mother, she was of no help to her hapless beaus. Gabriel had been one of the first to get into her mother's good graces and this because of his own highly evolved appreciation of the female form. On his first visit to their spacious Gracia flat, he had addressed her mother shockingly by her first name, and then, without a hint of hesitation, had discussed her dress with his usual combination of flattery and confidence. Since then, she had allowed him semi-unsupervised visits with her daughter, and never let him leave hungry.

Earlier in their relationship, Carme's words would have been an opening to an afternoon of kissing. Now, Gabriel only felt a mild panic, even as she pushed him away roughly and left. Carme proffered and withdrew herself with equal abandon, ordinarily a surefire tactic, but this time, Gabriel remained unmoved. He kicked at the ground as he watched her bike roll down the hazy street. What was he going to do? She was graduating from their snobby Parc Guell high school after this year and she wanted promises. Gabriel was quite sure he wasn't going to be able to keep any promises. Not if they involved not kissing other girls.

Carme was almost gone when he remembered another female figure receding in the distance. It was last year, on a family trip to India, on a bus. A Sikh man had been arguing with a blonde backpacker about playing her 'dirty' American music on the bus speaker system, and then taken it up with the driver. Gabriel's mother had been furious that the driver had let the passenger have his way and oust the girl from the bus. A compact vociferous force, Dr Mrs Deva had lectured both men in Hindi all the way to Delhi.

Unlike most teenagers, Gabriel wasn't mortified at this encounter. He wasn't even surprised that his mother knew Hindi, even though he had never heard either of his parents speak it. They usually spoke their native Tamil to each other, Spanish and Catalan to him and his brother, and English when they were angry. Anyway, his mother had always been this way, marching to the front and getting her way, defying authority and Appa at every turn.

At the time, Gabriel had only one desperate wish: to be back in Barcelona. He had pressed his forehead against the fissured bus window and tried to tamp down his arousal. Outside, the girl had been smiling, if bemusedly, despite her unceremonious offloading, her dusty figure slowly blending with the landscape as the bus drove away. Her sun-burned cheeks, glossed lips, and the song's husky moaning reminded him that he hadn't masturbated in days.

Touring around India with his parents had been hell, and not just because of the lack of privacy. He had hated being dragged from place to place, listening to interminable historical lectures, and not being able to wander as he wished. Gabriel wasn't used to being around his parents, because they both travelled extensively for work. His mother was a history professor with teaching posts in both England and Spain. This meant she was away more than not. When he and his brother had been younger, his father had been home every evening, but when Sailan left for college and Gabriel reached his teens, Appa had started travelling more to India, where he had expanded his business dealings.

Gabriel loved being left alone in his family's cluttered Eixample house, even though his parents' absences frequently left him hungry. They gave him a weekly food allowance which, unbeknownst to them, lasted half that time. Every Wednesday or so, Gabriel ran out of money, but he wasn't about to complain. The freedom was more than enough compensation.

After school or football practice, he'd race his bike to the sea as fast as he could. Ten humid kilometres from Parc Guell to the docks, lined with sycamores, all of it upwind, downhill. If he timed it right, he could be sliding over the sea with the sun still strong on his back. To save time, he had persuaded the girl who worked at the board shop to let him pay after, heaving, aching, hungry for more.

In any case, he could always find food. The pretty baker on the corner gave him day-old loaves for a few pesetas, or for free if she were feeling generous. The Pakistani butcher slipped him the heels of meat rolls, and old Señora Bailo next door could always be counted on to share the escudella stew she made every Sunday with her young hungry neighbour.

And there was always Carme's. Breaking up with her was going to be difficult. Gabriel had grown used to having dinner at her flat a few times a week after football practice. He had even been able to save some of his food allowance for the football shirt he wanted to buy Sailan for his birthday. Gabriel missed his brother. His whole family did. He guessed it was why his parents were away so often. Without Sailan to distract them from their differences, his parents were even more prone to argument than usual.

The first big fight Gabriel remembered was when his mother had been offered a teaching position at Harvard, a year before Sailan would apply. It had taken a prolonged and painful argument over the course of weeks to reveal the reasons behind his father's resistance. Not patriarchal or other traditional concerns, but a deep and obscurely reasoned distaste for the Americans. She had gone anyway, and Sailan had followed two years later.

Religion was another battleground. The Devas had left Madras in the sixties after getting married, and had jointly renounced Hinduism for a religion that appeared more matched to their new Spanish life: Catholicism. Adherence had lasted only a few years, despite their vague inclination towards faith and a mutual disregard for the hierarchies of Hinduism. Gabriel's father had lapsed into agnosticism while his mother had turned to a pick-and-choose version of Brahminism. Books on Kali and Krishna had been added to the overflowing shelves, but when his father balked at the small Ganesha shrine in the corner of the guest room, the truce was called off.

Gabriel liked the puja room. The smell of the incense was heady, and Ganesha wasn't behind bars and barbs, like some of the Gods he had seen on the streets in India. When he stared at the statue of the many-armed elephant God, he could tell it knew things he didn't. What might a God say about the sea? How did one learn the ways of the wind? Perhaps Ganesha would tell him, if only he'd concentrate a while longer, but, of course, Gabriel never could.

It was Sailan's indifference to the puja room that had finally put an uneasy end to the argument.

'Does it matter if there's a puja room or not?' he asked, his halting Tamil belying his cocksure manner.

'Of course it does,' their mother had burst out, her eyes wide. She was standing in the doorway of the puja room, her dupatta wrapped loosely about her neck, forming a makeshift hood. 'Isn't that the whole point? In the ritual of praying, you come closer to God.'

'All that blind faith and you'll drive me to atheism yet,' Appa said, his head buried in the refrigerator as he searched for leftovers.

'I don't see how my private actions affect your leftover principles,' their mother retorted.

Gabriel found the sound of Tamil comforting, despite everyone's raised tones.

'Exactly my point, Amma,' Sailan interrupted, switching to fluid Catalan. 'If you don't have a puja room, does it mean you don't believe?'

'No, of course not,' their father muttered in satisfaction, as he pried open a yoghurt tub filled with pallid vegetables.

'And if there is one,' Sailan turned to his father, 'does it mean you must have faith?'

In the silence following these pointed words, Gabriel felt as if something had been lost, but couldn't quite say what. He understood desire and ritual, and how physical expression could, in fact, create something out of nothing. What he wasn't sure about was what that meant. Moreover, with the new household moratorium on addressing religion openly, Ganesha now seemed less likely to speak to him. It was the first time Gabriel had doubted his older brother.

Sailan had always been the favoured child, the one with the quick, winning smile. He got stellar marks and kept his Catalan girlfriends and American pornography well out of sight. Gabriel, on the other hand, had no interest in pandering to his patronising teachers or his prudish parents. He also took very little personally. He knew his parents didn't approve of his interracial relationships, or really any relationships at all. His girlfriends' parents weren't thrilled either. Gabriel felt the regret sitting heavy on everyone's shoulders, but he didn't care. His life was an open book, much to everyone's chagrin.

Despite Sailan's status in the family, his last visit had been nothing short of disastrous. After leaving for Harvard, he had returned to Barcelona only once. During that visit, on his penultimate night home, he had walked into the house with some old school friends, and then ushered them upstairs hurriedly. Gabriel thought it was the smell in the house. Amma was cooking a pungently aromatic vegetable dish and a fresh pot of sambar. Sailan had never taken to Indian food, neither its spiciness nor its smell. For as long as Gabriel could remember, their normally belligerent mother had prepared separate dishes for her first-born, claiming it was due to Sailan's sensitive digestive system.

But it hadn't been the smell of Indian food that had offended Sailan. It was Appa. Gabriel had never considered their father's post-work rituals consciously until that day. Upon returning home, Appa would go upstairs and remove his suit, uniformly grey or navy, leave on a thin white singlet that stretched over his ballooning waist, and tie on a well-worn lungi. Downstairs, he would gather the newspapers from the hall table where his mother had discarded them, and get an apple from the kitchen. Then he'd squat in the corner of the living room, eat the apple, and read the papers. What was wrong with wearing pants? Sailan had asked. Or maybe squatting in the study instead of the living room?

'The study is crowded,' Appa said mildly, choosing to reply to the second query, combing through the few remaining hairs on top of his head.

'Because you use it for storage,' Sailan said.

Appa shrugged. 'There's enough space in the living room for all of us.'

'The space is not the point. We can't use the living room for entertaining. I'd just like to bring my friends over without feeling as if we're entering a television programme about displaced immigrants.'

It was true that their living room didn't look like any Catalan living room Gabriel had been in. The paisley print curtains didn't match the plastic-covered furniture, and there were piles of papers in all the corners. Appa had never cared for how things appeared, but his contempt for Sailan's tone overcame his disregard.

'We *are* displaced immigrants,' he said, in an

uncharacteristically sharp way. 'And I'm not sure how you remembered all these European manners after your years in the Land of the Free.'

'Why do you hate the States so? Amma goes all the time.'

'She goes so she can teach the Americans a thing or two.'

Sailan gave into the jibe. 'The US is not devoid of learning or etiquette.'

Not looking up from his newspaper, Appa said dryly, 'I'm glad to hear it, since we're paying so much money for you to learn the details. Like whether it might behoove you to respect your elders.'

Gabriel was relieved that this ended the conversation, because their mother had just appeared in the doorway to see what was going on, and there was no telling what would happen next.

Sailan had gone upstairs without another word and engaged with his family only peripherally for the rest of his stay. To Gabriel's great disappointment, their windsurfing plans went the way of Sailan's goodwill. The sport was his brother's old passion and it felt more natural than anything Gabriel had done so far. The sea, with its beckon and lull, mesmerized him. Windsurfing felt like flying, as if the sky were gathering him up into itself, the sea beating at his board from a deep distance below. Every brush of the wind meant something now, even when he wasn't near water. He could feel when there was rain in the air, when the breeze was too light or too heavy, when it was exactly right. Like the swinging light of a lighthouse, the wind marked his course along the sea. He had been eager to share this new understanding with Sailan.

Instead, the only solo time they got together was during the Barcelona–Sevilla game, lounging on the floor of the living room, eating pimientos out of a greasy paper bag. Gabriel wiped his hands on the tops of his feet and looked at his brother.

'Why are you wearing a kurta?' he asked. Sailan usually eschewed anything Indian.

'My clothes are being washed,' Sailan said and then shouted at the TV, 'What the fuck is he doing?'

'He should have passed, the half-brain,' Gabriel said. He was still wearing his sweaty football practice uniform. He hadn't changed in the hope that Sailan would ask him about his latest match. Perhaps then he could tell him he was the youngest striker in the team. Sailan had also been in the high school team, so he might be impressed. Gabriel was trying to follow his brother's lead in any way he could, and though he had neither Sailan's grace nor his grades, he was a natural athlete and a born flirt, both of which kept him in adequate social standing.

'Precisely,' Sailan had replied, hitting Gabriel's arm. It was the last word between them, and the last time they had seen each other that trip. Sailan left the house directly after the match to meet friends, and the next morning, long before Gabriel woke up, Amma had taken him to the airport.

The night before his next football match, Gabriel hadn't slept well. He had been hungry despite the five mayonnaise sandwiches he had had for dinner. He was thinking of the new girl a class above him with doll-blonde locks and pink cheeks. Actually, it was her heaviness that drew him. It made her breasts push out at the buttons of her shirt. He was pretty sure he would be well fed at her house. It was going to be difficult to win her over as an older boy was already pursuing her, but Gabriel wasn't worried. What he was worried about was Carme. She had called him late in the night, waking him.

'Come to my place, Gabriel,' she had said in

that arrogant way he had first loved and now resented. 'Come now and leave early. And I'll do it the way you want.'

'I can't, Carmita,' he replied, wondering what 'the way he wanted' was. In his short and eventful love life, Gabriel had usually had the lead. But with Carme, she was the scientist, coming up with evermore bizarre experiments each long hot afternoon. It was one of the reasons he hadn't been able to tear away yet. He was madly curious what she'd think up the next time.

'I'm wearing those stockings you like. And I have my mother's pearls. I have an idea.'

It was as if she already knew his plans for breaking up with her, and was trying to subvert them. And Gabriel hadn't learned how to say no, no matter the consequence. This time, the consequence was fatigue, and it would turn out to be transforming.

At the match, Gabriel got into a fight. Predictably, it started with Borja, a tall pudgy-faced boy two classes above him, sporting a poison streak. Gabriel had taken over Borja's field position and the older boy could not bear the indignity. His hatred had been obvious from the first moment they had met, and Gabriel had immediately offered him fodder in the form of insult. It had been a conscious decision. He often ignored the racial slurs his classmates threw his way, but responded to the physical slights, instantly and often to his own detriment. Still, his passion during these fights kept them infrequent.

But Gabriel knew that Borja would prefer to fight it out. He also knew he wouldn't survive a fight with Borja well. So he had to keep it verbal as long as possible. His teasing manners with girls had given Gabriel a certain notoriety at school, which kept most of his classmates at bay, slightly in awe. So his veiled taunts to Borja were usually greeted with laughter. But Gabriel was exhausted, and not in top form that day.

'Pussy whipped by Carme, coloured monkeyboy?' Borja's question broke into Gabriel's sleepy reverie. He was playing Gabriel's game, taking a Catalan moniker and twisting it, racial epithets Gabriel had heard before, though not in that combination. He would have appreciated the creativity coming from anyone else, but this was Borja. Plus, the boy had accompanied his sneer with a push. Gabriel reacted before he could think: a sweep of his dead fast right foot, his body weight landing squarely on Borja's solar plexus, and an ill-advised rejoinder.

'At least I have pussywhip. Whiter than anything you'll ever smell.'

Despite Gabriel's force and quickness, his weight was no match for Borja's. Nor did his brief anger come close to Borja's purpling. Borja went straight for his face and Gabriel barely had time to sacrifice his cheek to save his nose. Moments later, when the coach tore them apart, he was bleeding, his lip swollen, teeth outlined in red, eye blackening, doubled over in pain. Borja, on the other hand, stood upright, breathing heavily, florid and stolid as ever.

It was the last straw for the Devas. The letters from Gabriel's teachers had always been a steady stream, though they allowed that his marks reflected little on his abilities. The reports noted his inventive participation. It was just that no one could depend on him to submit his homework. Given the latest, the teachers were quick to stress their original judgement: Gabriel was bad news.

His parents had exhausted two private schools in Barcelona and, finally, their patience. The verdict was crushing. Gabriel was to leave

Spain and be enrolled in a military-run school in the States. Sailan would check up on him mid-semester, and his mother in the winter.

Gabriel begged his parents to let him stay, to defend him to the school, but to no avail.

'This is where I belong, Amma, Appa,' he said desperately. 'Don't you see? It doesn't matter what anyone says, least of all that thug Borja.' He spat out the name.

'Barcelona doesn't seem to want you,' his father said not unsympathetically, even as his wife silenced him with a look.

'Gabriel, you've been enough trouble already,' she said, as Gabriel's heart sank. His mother had switched to English. She would brook no further argument. 'How much money have we spent sending you to these schools?'

'But America, Appa?' he appealed to his father, who hesitated. 'I dream in Catalan,' he continued, hating the plaintiveness in his voice.

'You can still dream in Catalan over there,' his mother said, picking up her reading glasses, the conversation over.

Gabriel's last meeting with Carme was not as brutally brief. While it offered him his last Catalan love in his favourite tilted tunnel in Parc Guell, he was too distraught to enjoy it. They were leaning against one of the slant pillars of the tunnel, an intuitive angle for illicit activities. The inside of the tunnel seemed to him a wave made of smooth stone, curling inexorably, on the verge of annihilation.

'But it's perfect!' she said in between tender, carefully placed kisses. Gabriel's injuries were not trivial. 'I'm going to university in America. I'll be there in just a few months. We can be together again.'

'Carme, don't you understand? It's not an ordinary school. I can't just leave when I wish.' Gabriel only faintly appreciated the out he was getting from his relationship with Carme. There was far too much sitting on the other scale. He felt the imbalance bodily, the weight sending him ricocheting off Barcelona, away from the sea.

A week later, Gabriel was on a plane. As the take-off roar sounded, he glanced out of the window and was startled to see his reflection. Blue-black hair curving over a matching blue-black eyelid. Lower lip still too fat to close his mouth properly. Dull red cut healing unevenly on his cheek. Maybe the rough look would keep everyone away long enough for him to find his place. His throat contracted when he thought of where he was going. He knew nothing about the school except that it had no football, no girls, and most distressingly, no aquamarine sea nearby.

Gabriel looked again inside the satchel on his lap. His boarding pass for his second-ever flight lay on top, this one heading west. Underneath the ticket, folded carefully, was Sailan's Barca football shirt. Sailan was meeting him at the airport in Washington D.C. and driving him to his new school in Virginia. His brother had sounded smoothly angry on the phone. Gabriel's stunt, as he called it, was making him miss four classes and an interview. He had had to ask his roommate Raza to help pick up the slack. Maybe Gabriel would wait to give him the shirt, so it didn't look like a peace offering. He closed his satchel and placed it under the seat.

CAREFUL, BABY

he stands to her right
lit by old gold light
light in which to see the bride
before this faded afternoon
in the winter of them
past the sexinanynewplace stage
but still, one kiss
and the touch of his tongue is
a new new thing
again

Modhu sat in her lilac dining room, alone. Her husband had never liked the colour, but she hadn't cared until now. That he might not ever remark, with distaste or not, on the wallpaper and carefully matched lampshades, all specially ordered from Modhu's high-end furniture shop in Dhaka, seemed overwhelming. She spread her hand delicately across her embroidered silk sari, arching the finger wearing the diamond eternity ring, a gift from her last wedding anniversary. That was the night everything had started to go wrong. At the time, she had seen it as a beginning of sorts, a way out of her growing misery. She hadn't known that she would come to long for that state of mind. That she would wish for the time her inner life was hers alone, no matter how lonely.

Her phone rang and she felt the old thrill before it was stanched by dread. She looked at the screen. It was Billi, a gossipy friend. Probably back from the Sonargaon reception, wanting to talk. Modhu couldn't speak to her. She didn't know if she could speak at all. She felt a wave of nausea, something that had been happening more often lately. For a moment, she entertained the notion that she might be pregnant. The nausea increased in intensity at the thought. No, she was sure it was something else. It was probably the shrimp at the reception. She could never resist eating shrimp despite her allergy. One, and her cheeks would bloom in a not-unattractive manner. Two, and her throat started itching, her tongue thickening. Three and, well, she hadn't gone that far since she was a child.

Tonight, she had stopped after one plump prawn, coated in lime juice and salt. She had needed all her concentration to look natural during the furious whispered fight she and Shagor had had by the Sonargaon pool. She had done it too. Even when he had grabbed her arm, pressing her thick black pearl bangle painfully against her wrist, she had leaned into him languidly, whispering, sing-song, 'Careful, baby...'

Shagor had abruptly remembered himself and let her go, self-consciously straightening his exquisitely tailored suit. For all his new-money brashness, and he was unashamed of it, Shagor knew style. It was that brand of unashamedness she had fallen for, the way he had walked into her life assuming she wanted him. And she had. But it hadn't been easy, marrying someone this literal, this direct. Nothing in her ignore-the-problem-and-it-will-go-away upbringing had prepared her for the loud-mouthed-say-everything brand of communication that Shagor practised. They had learned to communicate somewhere in between those boundaries, and in doing so, had changed each other indefinably. Modhu had a feeling her influence had not been the generous one, but it wasn't easy transforming a lifetime of muteness.

Shagor had sent her home from Sonargaon, saying they would talk about the whole bloody thing later. She hated it when he used British slang when he felt at the end of his rope. As if some thin-lipped colonial expletive would properly express the seriousness of his emotion. She hated even more that she'd obeyed him and returned to their house full of echoing rooms. It was her guilt, she knew. Not just about betraying Shagor, but about not seeing it all coming. Not keeping her world under control as she had always been able to. Not being able to resist Seku.

Modhu had always liked Seku. He had old-fashioned bideshi manners that somehow didn't irritate her the way Shagor's did. Perhaps because Seku's Britishisms were delivered with flirtatious charm. She had liked his wife, Nita, even more. Nita was the breadwinner of that family. With her high-profile bank job, and numerous smaller enterprises on the side, it was surprising how silly and fun she was. She had a guffawing laugh that shook her ample body all over. Seku would sometimes spontaneously lean over, grab her by her upper arms and kiss her soundly. If Modhu hadn't been embarrassed by the display of affection, she would have wanted to do the same to Nita. She inspired that kind of emotion.

They had first met Seku and Nita at a dinner party at another friend's house, years ago. The maid of the house, a feisty woman called Komola, had stood proudly in the dining room until she was given thanks for the meal she had cooked.

Over the innumerable delicacies on the table, the four of them had been introduced and got along from the beginning, laughing through dinner and the hours following. Their friendship had continued at Modhu and Shagor's house, even while Nita and Seku's relationship slowly disintegrated. It was only after Nita's daughter, Ila, was born that Nita had stopped coming over, citing motherhood, exhaustion, career, anything that kept that distance.

Seku still came over occasionally, and they talked as passionately around the table, but they laughed less. And when Shagor started travelling more, leaving Modhu and Seku on their own, the conversations became even more serious. In a way, Modhu felt as if she were being banished back to her childhood, silence taking over an empty house again.

Part of the reason she felt she was in a time warp was that she was once again living in her sprawling childhood home. After her mother had died, a host of property disputes had forced them to leave their Gulshan flat and move to Dhanmondi. She and Shagor only used the ground floor and had closed off the second floor. The walls had been repainted, the curtains changed and windows opened up, but it was difficult for Modhu to stop remembering the old days.

In her childhood days, Dhanmondi had been closer to its namesake, an actual dhan khet, replete with ankle-twisting foxholes and skin-scraping burrs. It hadn't prevented her brother from endlessly exploring the fields with his friends. Modhu longed to follow him despite her fear of the foxes, but she was usually required to sit at home and read. Their mother had contracted a permanent headache after their father had passed away, and a suffocating quiet enveloped the days and nights. Guests were rarely invited and no visiting children were allowed to disturb the peace.

Modhu switched off the lamp, and the triangle of violet light vanished with the rest of the room. The house was empty as the maid only came in the mornings. She walked to the kitchen and pushed open the back door, letting in the cool night air. A thread from her anchal snagged on the latch and she rescued it before it ripped. She had been catching her clothes on this latch for as long as she could remember.

She remembered a summer day, long ago. Her brother had persuaded their mother to let him go to a friend's house for lunch, and Modhu had jealously watched him leave. She waited until her mother was in her room, and then crept out of the back door. As she ducked past the windows, she saw her brother's new bicycle leaning against the wall. She knew how to ride a bicycle because her father had taught her before he died, but hers was far too small now, and her brother's was too big. Still, its gleaming body and red seat beckoned. She wheeled it silently out of the compound into the field.

When the path through the fields turned out to be too bumpy for a comfortable ride, Modhu steered through the waving grass, fronds as tall as she was, into the street. Part of the problem was that she was too short to position herself over the crossbar and still reach the pedals. So her body was part way under the bar, which allowed her to reliably, though awkwardly, pedal, even if she couldn't settle on the seat. Once on the street, she was finally able to pick up speed. If she squinted, her peripheral vision of the trees and storefronts blurred into the road, and the wind became everything. Even the dank gutter of refuse to her left, slowly bubbling its way backwards, receded.

By the time Modhu heard the honking, it

was too late to stop safely. A massive blue and yellow truck had just turned the corner and was barrelling down the road towards her. It couldn't have taken more than a second to make her choice, but to Modhu, the moment lasted ages. She looked at the bubbling black water ditch and at the crayon-coloured truck, and made her move.

When she emerged from the gutter, dragging the bicycle with her, Modhu thought she would die of disgust. She was so thoroughly coated with gutter filth that the red of the bike seat and the yellow of her dress were the same dark ooze. And she wasn't even quite sure where she was. Ignoring an offer of help from a teashop owner, who was making no effort to conceal his hacking amusement, she climbed on the bike and headed back. Her sandals were slippery with gunk and she slipped off the pedals more than once, banging her already bruised legs.

When she got to the corner, she recognized where she was. Fairly far from home, but she knew where she could go. There was a pond a kilometre away, half swallowed by lily pads. It was too small for regular washing and bathing and there were too many trees around it to enable a helpful bank, so it had become the domain of the local street children.

Luckily, when Modhu got there, it was deserted, as most street kids were either working or begging. She gratefully dunked herself and the bike into the murky green water, submerging herself for as long as she could. The mud at the base of the pond felt suspiciously like the gutter slime, but the water was instantly refreshing. As soon as she could see her skin again, Modhu sat in the sun to dry off and inspect her wounds. Nothing serious. One scrape on her shin, two on her arms. They would heal quickly, and she would just have to wear a long-sleeved dress for a few days. She peered at her distorted reflection on the chrome frame of the bicycle. Her hair was a mess, but her face looked unhurt. And, thank God, the bike appeared to be fine. When she was dry, she could go home, and no one would be the wiser.

Modhu had told Shagor this story soon after their wedding. They were lying on two lounge chairs in a tiny balcony in their first apartment, waiting for the afternoon heat to dissipate. Two ancient tamarind trees protected them from direct sunlight, but Modhu could see beads of sweat forming on Shagor's forehead. A curl of smoke unwound from the mosquito coil burning at their feet. It had been left untouched for hours and was dropping tiny bricks of ash in a spiral around its disappearing self.

'So your mother never said anything?' Shagor asked, lacing his fingers through hers lazily. His palms were damp, but she ignored that and traced the length of his fingers.

'No, I don't think she ever found out about that incident.' Modhu laughed. 'My brother might have guessed something had happened, but he didn't ask. God, I still remember how repulsive falling into that gutter felt!'

'No, I mean in general. She didn't talk to you?'

'She did talk. Just not much.' Remembering her mother's recent death, weeks before the wedding, made Modhu's throat tighten. They had rushed the event, planning it in the middle of the monsoon season, in the hope that she would make it, but it was not to be. Her cancer had been too far gone. The lightness that the gutter story had wrought ebbed from her voice. She wished they would change the subject, but Shagor seemed oblivious.

'She sounds like the opposite of my mother,'

he said lightly, bringing her hand to his mouth to kiss it.

'Your family can't stop talking,' Modhu said, more sharply than she meant to.

'It's better than not talking at all!' Shagor said, obviously stung. 'Anyway, I was just going to say that—'

'We do, I mean, did talk,' Modhu interrupted, although it wasn't ordinarily her nature. 'Just not about everything as soon as it happens.'

'I was just going to say,' Shagor repeated gently, 'that you can talk to me about anything you like. And as soon as it happens too.'

'It's not the way I do things,' she said, feeling ungracious even as she said it, but unable to stop. 'But I'll try,' she amended.

Modhu *had* tried. But it seemed Shagor had no sense of how much it cost her. The secret thoughts, the deep-down fears, the slightly scandalous requests, he treated her revelations the same way he'd respond to a question about what to eat that night. It was difficult for Modhu to get used to the casual way he did everything. She found herself holding back when she was not feeling up to a careless answer. Sometimes, Shagor noticed her hesitations, pressed her into a conversation. She was surprised to realize that she appreciated his efforts even though they were as likely to end in laughter as not. But as their work schedules became increasingly involved, these semi-forced intimacies became less frequent, and Modhu reverted to her old, aloof ways. Her regret over their tenuous connection was gradually replaced by relief at not having to stretch so far outside her lines.

It was Seku, Shagor's best friend, who had picked up on the missing pieces, Modhu's carefully couched confidences. When it was just the two of them alone at the dining table, every pause lengthened. The silence threatened to outline the shapes of their missing partners, and rather than remember them, they rushed to fill it, first with talking, and then with touching.

It was on her fourth wedding anniversary that Modhu took on her second lover. A thunderstorm was slowly submerging the city when Shagor called from Shanghai to tell her that he would not be celebrating with her. He had been due back later that day, but problems with the manufacturing unit were holding him back, possibly through the weekend. From the newly glass-walled veranda, she called the restaurant to cancel the reservations she had made more than a month ago. Then she sank into a leather armchair and watched the rain.

Seku had called so soon afterwards that she hadn't had time to make up a good story, and was angry enough not to avoid the topic. She responded to his congratulations with ill-restrained vitriol towards marriage, husbands, and love.

By the time she got to men, Seku interrupted, 'Okay, while it might be true that we are unthinking bastards, it's also true that we don't bake the whole pie of reprobation ourselves. Sometimes, women get a slice or two.'

Modhu briefly considered Seku's own loveless life, but then plowed on, 'I'm not interested in sharing the blame right now.'

'I understand totally. Would you, however, be interested in sharing a bottle of wine? I have some wonderful Shiraz I just smuggled back from Sydney.'

'Bring it over then.'

Modhu rarely drank more than a glass of wine at a time, and then only with a heavy meal at a dinner party. Having never gotten really tipsy, she was surprised at how pleasant it was. And how easily she was able to put Shagor out of mind when just a few hours ago she had been unable to stop obsessing for a second.

The watery light filtered into the veranda as Seku recounted stories of school pranks and thwarted boyhood love. As evening set in, they moved into the kitchen where Modhu fried up onion boras and squeezed limes for sherbet. She loved cooking and had never kept a cook, even though Shagor had not wanted his wife in the kitchen.

She was no longer drunk when she first leaned towards Seku to kiss him. She was languorous, a little fatigued perhaps, but perfectly in control of her senses. Seku, on the other hand, had maintained his intoxication with tumblers of Shagor's expensive scotch. Still, he was the one who moved away, but so slowly that he didn't break contact for a few seconds.

Modhu touched her wine-red lips, wondering at herself. Looking up and away from Seku, she unexpectedly laughed out loud. The fan spun slowly, moving the heavy air-conditioned air through the living room. Seku watched her, unsure of her mood. When she leaned in again, eyes narrowed, her hand trailing along the velvet cushions, he did not resist.

Modhu wasn't sure why she had told Shagor about her affair with Seku. It was clear to her that it was over between them anyway. Seku had stopped calling her months ago, after a torrid heart-stopping year. He had given no warning, but she wasn't surprised. It was a gift, she had thought, each time their affair flared into being, each hour they kissed without stopping. But it was also empty, in the way only affairs can be. Still, Modhu had gone through the usual cycles of blame, despair, regret, defensiveness, loneliness, and relief, sometimes all at once. She wasn't over it, but she knew she was close.

Maybe that was the reason she had pulled Shagor aside from the glittering wedding guests to tell him her final, fatal confidence. Her life was about to return to a dead space where nothing moved forward, or backward. Perhaps her subconscious was trying to prevent that with this sabotaging and self-defeating move. Besides, she was tired of lying, no matter how inconveniently timed this confessional urge was.

Would Shagor understand the isolation that had driven her into another man's arms, dispel it with a sweep of his easy manner? If not, would Seku return when he heard that she was alone? She knew these were hopeless hopes, but she could not guess what would happen, and more disturbingly, she wasn't sure what she wanted to happen. She was even past wishing the affair had never happened, that she and Shagor could go back to their old life.

The front door opened and Modhu froze. Shagor walked down the long hallway leading to the kitchen. Still unable to move, she felt a strange pain awaken in her belly, and slowly move into her pelvis.

'I'm leaving,' Shagor said.

The pain increased sharply. The last person she had made love to was Shagor, two months ago. It had been hurried as he was late for his latest business trip, but sweeter than usual. Modhu had been feeling especially vulnerable that day, having just recently understood that she and Seku were finished. She had decided not to go to her shop that morning, and was lying on the bed, flipping through a new Dhaka glossy magazine. Shagor had sat down beside her unexpectedly. She had thought for a moment that he could sense her emotion, but then he had started telling her about the problems with his upcoming meeting.

Modhu had gathered herself with some effort.

'You can try to arrange a meeting beforehand with the factory manager,' she had responded.

He had absently played with the ruffle on her nightie. When his hand brushed past her breast, Modhu had visibly seen him switch gears.

'Basically…' he had said, the meeting all but forgotten, 'all I wanted to say was that you're beautiful.'

She had smiled, despite her distress, and he had kissed her, and kissed her again.

'I can't stand this empty house anymore,' Shagor said, his voice disembodied in the darkness. 'We shouldn't have moved here. Your brother should have had it. He would have made better use of it anyway, with his pack of brats.'

Modhu knew then that Shagor was deeply hurt. He had always wanted kids, so he would never make light of the issue. The pain surrounded her womb with frightening urgency. Something in her body let go. She summoned all her strength to speak, even though she didn't know what to say.

'I love you,' she said, in a surprisingly steady voice.

He was silent, and then replied, 'I don't see that, Modhu.'

'Don't leave,' she said, startling herself again.

She had no idea where these words were coming from. Actually, she did. It was desperation. But she didn't know how her pride had let the words loose. Perhaps the same tremor that was pulling her baby from her body.

'I cannot stay,' Shagor said. 'Not here. Not with you.'

Standing in the doorway, her fingers on the old latch, Modhu closed her eyes, remembering her near-accident on the bike, more than twenty years ago. Blood had started slipping down thickly between her legs, dripping down the step onto the ground. She was leaning so hard on the latch that it was cutting into her palm. Her legs were somehow keeping her upright, despite her now intense fatigue. In her mind's eye, she could see her choices with perfect clarity, the dusty road, the brightly painted truck with its horn blaring, the black gutter focusing to the side.

The blood was now pooling in the dusty grass. Everything was dry, so dry. She would have to remember to water the garden in the morning. Modhu released her grip on the latch and let the door close.

WAX DOLL

a drop is born
it gathers
weight, fullness
until the moment
it is roundest

then, motion
a liquid interior
breaks through the skin
comes forth
sliding itself down
inside out
till it disappears

Ila was sitting in her father's dining room, surrounded by the remains of dinner. The heat of the summer was as liquid a presence as rain, though it hadn't rained during the day. Her t-shirt was dark with sweat, but she was determined not to switch on the air conditioner. It was her new rule because she hated the transition from dry cold AC air into real Dhaka. Instant wilt. Like a momer putul, a little wax doll, her Nana would say fondly. Without the AC, Ila was only half-listless all the time, instead of bouncing between two extremes. Still, she insisted on the heat, even as her spiked-up hair got less edgy by the hour.

'The last thing anyone should want nowadays,' her mother was saying, 'is a love marriage.'

Her father retorted, 'No one does arranged marriages anymore. Not unless there's a mullah in the immediate family. There's certainly not one in ours.' He swilled his glass of wine meaningfully and winked at Ila.

Ila found herself silently agreeing with her mother. She knew what havoc love could wreak. Her own parents had been estranged her entire life, despite a beginning that boasted of true love. So many people had told Ila that her parents had been considered *the* example of a love marriage. Nita and Seku's affectionate and humorous exchanges were still remembered decades later. One story took place at a wedding, long before Ila was born. Her mother's anger at her father's late arrival had turned into helpless laughter when he appeared with two large, blooming irises. With a solemn face, he first affixed one flower behind his ear, and then with exaggerated care placed the other behind hers. Others spoke of how their every encounter began and ended with a kiss.

Ila couldn't quite see her decorous father kissing anyone in public. And she didn't remember her parents not fighting, or worse, when they renounced fighting for a louder sort of silence. Her mother first started leaving her father, when Ila was a baby, in an increasing whirlwind of business trips, each one taking her farther away, for longer and longer. Her father countered by having an affair with Modhu Aunty, the wife of his best friend, Shagor Uncle, capping another love marriage gone wrong.

When her mother immigrated to America, she had taken Ila with her, leaving her father heartbroken and alone. Ila could see the years on his face, still elegant but lined. He was the only reason she had stopped kicking and screaming. When her mother pulled her out just before her last year of high school in America, dragging her back to Bangladesh, she had originally felt as if she had died, or arrived on another planet. Once Ila realized that her mother wasn't going to budge, she set herself to finding her Dhaka groove. Her father's unrestrained joy at their return was her first and favourite track.

'Did you hear Modhu's daughter has divorced her husband?' her mother exclaimed. 'They only got married a few months ago. And she was outrageously young anyway.'

Ila's father looked shocked but said nothing. Ila didn't know if it was the mention of Modhu Aunty, or the split. Neither of her parents were close to Modhu Aunty or Shagor Uncle anymore, not since the affair. And even though the other couple had got back together, and even had a kid soon after, it had never seemed easy again.

'The guy she married was a chhagol!' Ila said, more to deflect the conversation than anything. 'I don't know what Shurobhi saw in him.'

'She was in love,' said her mother. 'You know, that virus infecting everyone these days.'

Ila laughed. 'What I don't get is why she looked so sad even at the wedding. It's like the old days, when brides had to look in mirrors and cry their eyes out.'

'Or maybe it was the weight of seven sets of jewellery,' her mother said, pressing her ample cleavage, as if weighed down. 'Modhu always did go gaga on the plumage, so her daughter would too.'

This time, even Ila flinched, and her mother finally stopped her tirade. She knew her mother was not being herself. Ordinarily light-hearted

and funny, even silly, she turned brittle and hard
around Ila's father. These weekly dinners were
a strain and Ila wished her mother would stop
trying, just let Ila eat with each of them separately,
in peace.

But now, Ila was afraid of other things, afraid
for all the rose-blinded couples unable to see the
love-propelled disaster descending upon them,
afraid for her own chances at marital joy. She
wasn't going to get married just to get divorced.
She knew how hard it was, even when you loved
someone to pieces. She was going to be prepared.

Ila met the jilting bride in question a few
weeks later at a garden party. Shurobhi was
decked out, as lavishly as befitted a newly-wed,
but with none of the attendant diffidence.
Chain-smoking through a pack of Bensons, she
ignored all the whispering aunties and invited
Ila to sit with her.

'Should we talk about my divorce and get it
over with?' Shurobhi said, arching her pencil-thin
eyebrows. She was several years younger than Ila,
but had a poise that belied it.

Ila smiled, winding her anchal around her
shoulders to keep the evening insects at bay.
'Only if you want to. Because I think I already

have the scoop, just from walking through the garden of gossip.'

'Okay, fine. I know divorces can ruin you, especially if you're a woman,' Shurobhi said, 'but at least it means you're not trapped for the rest of your life.'

'True,' Ila replied, unsure if she should say anything else. She didn't want to offend Shurobhi, but she had her own take on this from her experience as a child of divorced parents. She continued, 'But in the old days, you had to fight tooth and nail to get into a love marriage, and it usually lost you everything else. So you'd have to really want someone to go through all that trouble, you'd have to choose carefully. And God forbid you picked poorly, because after all the hassle, who'd want to walk away? Who could?'

'So what's your point? People aren't choosing carefully now?' Shurobi looked unconvinced.

'Yes! Because it's so much easier now to have love. People pick carelessly and then – making it worse – they don't try as hard. Maybe they think the love bit will take care of the rest. But it won't.'

'And the solution is you let someone else choose your husband for you? But who chooses?

Your divorced parents?' Shurobhi asked pointedly.

'Good point. I'm not sure actually,' Ila admitted. 'Anyway, I'll vet my beaus a little bit. I'm just saying I'm not going to look too closely, especially after the wedding. I'm going to make do with my lot. Make it happen the old-fashioned way. The way it worked for my grandparents and their grandparents.'

'Okay, you turn a blind eye. I'm going to check back with you in ten years when you're stuck with some phorsha fool.' The edge in Shurobhi's voice was softened by what sounded like pity.

Ila smiled even as she shook her head. She was going to make her own marriage work, through quips or quiescence, one way or another. Prayers by a paynim. After all, Ila still performed the Maghreb prayer. It was the only one she did now, though she used to do all five when she was younger, when her mother left, when her father was left behind. When she thought it might bring them back together. She only prayed this last one now because she was unwilling to totally give up hope, in either God or her parents.

'Come over sometime, Shurobhi,' Ila said, finding herself genuinely wanting Shurobhi to do that. 'In fact, come next Saturday to my dad's flat in Gulshan. My best friend Rox is visiting from America. You can meet her. She's a riot.'

Shurobhi smiled, tipping her lipstick-stained cigarette from bejewelled fingers. 'That'd be nice.'

When Shurobhi came over for lunch, Ila and Rox were already drunk. Ila poured out an opaque tumbler of her father's wine and handed it over to Shurobhi jauntily.

'Ila, your hair looks good long,' Rox was saying. 'I can't remember the last time you grew it out.'

'I'm glad you mentioned that,' Shurobhi said, 'because I was wondering what the deal was with the American do.' She drawled out the word American.

Ila laughed, wringing her hair like a mop and releasing it. 'I'm just trying to play the good Bangladeshi girl. You know, so I can land a good Bangladeshi boy.'

'Forget it. There's none out there,' Shurobhi said.

'Not one?' asked Rox in disappointment. 'What about that boy whose photos your mom showed us? He looks cute.'

'Tahsin. Yeah, my mother loves his parents, and him,' said Ila with a twist of her mouth. 'We stayed with his family when we first moved back to Bangladesh.'

'I've known Tahsin since we were kids,' Shurobhi said, amused. 'You like him, Ila?'

'I've only talked to him a few times.' Ila found herself embarrassed without knowing why. To change the subject, she picked up the sports page and intoned heavily, 'Oh... oh, it was not easy for the skipper to "*accept*" the fact that he was no longer... captain.' She whispered the last word.

Rox started to shake in silent laughter. It was one of their oldest forms of entertainment, Ila's naturally hoarse voice at once mimicry, seduction, and melodrama. And the sports pages of Bangladesh newspapers displayed a kind of emotion and exuberance that was perfect for this purpose.

'What shocked me most was the way I was treated!' Ila switched to a high-pitched socialite's whine, and jumped up, pressing her hands against her heart. She pranced up the dining room, her dupatta trailing behind her, hair syncopating with her motion. When she turned, both Rox and Shurobhi were watching her intently. Her heart lurched with the same lost feeling she'd had before leaving America.

Dropping to her knees before Rox, Ila told her one version of the truth.

'I pitch before you, skipper mine.' Her hands cupped Rox's shoulders. 'My wicket heart has no chance against you. Give us a kiss.'

Rox obliged. She leaned down and pressed her lips against Ila's.

Ila was the first to break away, pounding heart, ribboned breath.

'Lovely,' Shurobhi said, clapping. 'Let's have another glass of Seku Uncle's wine and then we can go see your future husband.'

'What? Who?' Ila said, feeling paper thin and transparent.

'Tahsin. He's having a party at his place, except of course they call it an orgy.'

'An orgy?' Ila said, feeling even denser.

'Don't worry, they're not really,' Shurobhi said, lighting a cigarette. 'I mean, there's drinking, smoking, even hooking up. But not like sex or anything. More's the pity. But come on.'

The rain was coming, pressing the failing heat aside. The air sailed between tranquil and tumult, as the three of them banged out of the sprawling flat. The front door was a wrought Balinese gem that her mother had brought back on one of her business trips. It writhed with animal carvings that made Ila feel that the door was alive. Her father kept large leafy plants on either side of the entrance, creating the illusion of jungle-pounce even more potent.

They skipped down the marbelized stairs, into the rising wind. Rox and Ila were holding hands, half-running, half-screaming as the rain made its first sweep, spattering Ila's grey kameez black. Halfway down the next street, cowering under an obscenely pregnant jackfruit tree, Rox, and even the normally reserved Shurobhi, couldn't stop laughing.

'Ila, I don't know what it is about you,' Shurobhi said, lighting a cigarette as the wind pulled the rain down and around. 'Your hair, your face, your ability to get wet in a second, but you are straight out of a Bollywood film.'

Ila looked at herself. Her ordinary kameez and fine lace dupatta had become a dark mould of her body. Her hair, usually a surging mass around her shoulders, lay in thick parsed strands plastered around her face. She pushed a strand aside self-consciously, aware she was only unreeling the scene.

'No wonder the boys all want...' Shurobhi exhaled the words through the smoke.

Ila opened her mouth to protest, and Rox put a finger on her lips, shushing her. 'You only have to speak with that melty wax doll voice of yours, and we'll all be goners. Cholo.'

They resumed their push-pull stumbling run through the rain. At Tahsin's mansion of a house, Shurobhi kicked off her sandals into a pile of shoes in the foyer and ascended the gleaming granite stairs. Rox followed, as Ila prised her shoes off more slowly, stepping on the curled toes and letting them spring back. She looked up to see the maid, who had opened the door, standing there watching her.

'How are you, Komola?' she asked.

The last time she had talked to Komola was when Ila's mother had whisked Ila away from America. Ila hadn't realized her mother was serious about coming back to Bangladesh in the beginning, even when she had gone to Dhaka on her own first to find a flat for them. That was when Ila's mother had struck up a friendship with the maid, Tahsin's beloved nanny of twenty years. It was only when her mother came back to Baltimore to get Ila that it had sunk in. The flat hadn't been ready, so they lived in Tahsin's bougainvillea-draped house for a few months.

When they arrived from the airport, Ila's mother and Komola had greeted each other like old friends, laughing and hugging, but then when Ila and her mother were alone in the bedroom, Komola came in weeping. They tried to comfort her, but the maid was inconsolable. Ila didn't understand much of the garbled story. It was about Komola's husband, a love marriage it seemed. But there was something about his strange eyes, and another wife. A contract made, a contract broken. And Ila guessed this last part: finding love, and then losing it. Ila thought it may have never been there to begin with. Not real love anyway, the kind that made you stay, no matter what.

Komola shrugged tiredly. 'Asi toh. I'm here, as I've always been.'

Ila had no response. What could she say in the face of such exhaustion? She squeezed Komola's arm. It was unexpectedly soft.

Komola patted her back, and then said in a brighter voice, 'But my sister, July, has returned, by the grace of God! From India, though I did not even know where she had been all these years. I thought I would never see her again, but God had other plans. We cannot know what is written in our fates. We must not know, or else we would not be able to bear it! Life is very long.'

Ila was preoccupied as she ascended the stairs, the floor cool under her wet feet. She stopped outside Tahsin's room, where raucous voices were filtering out through the half-open door. She could hear Shurobhi introducing Rox around. There were people lounging on Tahsin's enormous bed and on the rug that lay on the floor below, lined with pillows. Most of the faces were familiar, but there was a man she didn't recognize leaning against the far wall. He was older than the rest of them and wearing a rain-stained kurta. She remembered her clothes drenched against her body and pulled at her kameez uncomfortably. When she looked up again, she saw him watching her. Before she could respond, something, a kind of understanding, passed between them. It had nothing to do with words, nor even with feelings.

She took in a deep breath and pushed open the door. A pop tarantella was playing on the Bose speakers. The room fell silent for a second, and before anyone could greet her, she put a finger to her lips dramatically. Snapping her fingers in time, she glided into the room in a spurious version of the tango, arms akimbo. She paused near Rox and vogued. Rox whooped, taking on the snapping rhythm.

'Are you ready for it?' Ila asked the room huskily. Voices chimed in assent. She noticed Tahsin draped over a chair by the stereo, inhaling from a joint, his chiselled face engaged. Ila clapped her hands down on her thighs and proceeded to smack different parts of her body.

'Is it the macarena?' someone called out as Ila kicked one leg out and then another, at odd, hooked angles. Rox jumped up beside Ila and followed her lead, fumblingly.

'No, it's the makorsha!' Ila spiked her clawed hands in the air, spider-like.

Waterdrops flung themselves from her swinging hair. Her backup dancer collapsed, laughing. Ila couldn't look in the stranger's direction for fear she'd fly apart. She didn't know why. She couldn't look at Rox either. So she looked at Tahsin, who hadn't stopped watching her since she had entered the room.

'Ila,' he said, 'how do you come up with this shit? It's hysterical.'

She shrugged, smiling, and sat down beside Shurobhi. A dance party had started up. The tarantella transitioned into an electronically remixed baul song.

'If nothing else, Tahsin has a stellar music collection,' Shurobhi whispered in her ear.

It was true, but not quite fair, Ila thought. Tahsin had much more than a hard drive full of eclectic MP3s. He also had a witty tongue, generous habits, and an unfailing charm with women. Which included every female from his terrorizing grandmother to Komola, his protective ayah.

The sun was burning its way through the rain clouds, though the air-conditioned house didn't give a hint of the heat. Rox was still gyrating to the music, and had pulled others into her orbit, including the stranger. He was older than Ila had first thought, maybe in his thirties or older. His eyelids were dark and his frame too thin. But she liked the lines around his eyes, his clinging kurta, his pricking presence. Someone flashed a million-watt smile at him, and Ila felt a clawing in her chest.

'He's an artist,' Shurobhi said into her ear.

'Who?' she said carelessly, though she knew perfectly well.

'Oyon. Tahsin's older brother. Has the best yabba hookups. He's crazy too.'

The stranger was next to her now, his bent of body inviting hers. She stilled herself to stone. She had always had trouble staying inside herself. In the time that followed, she became acutely conscious of every movement, in their bodies and within the room. Her skin prickled with each lean in and brush past, all intimated offerings. The hair on her neck stood up and she struggled to control her breathing, her heart.

The stranger traced a strand of Ila's hair. She was unable to keep herself together. When he took her arm, Ila barely felt his touch. Or she felt it too much. Her legs dissolved into the charged air, yet somehow she found herself standing by him, now dancing. He stood behind her, his arms lengthening along hers. Rox swayed in front of her, her palm pressing the damp flatness of Ila's stomach, her face achingly close.

Ila wanted to know if it were possible to want two opposite things at once, passion and reason, each growing fruit and fruit-eating serpents in her garden. Even before the game started, there were so many ways to lose. She wanted to remain in the moment, wanted it to last, wanted to remember forever what this felt like, to stand between the old and the new, both urgent, neither tenable.

As the music segued again, this time to a trance samba number, the stranger moved away. Ila knew the moment was lost, no one else's but hers to recall. Her legs took shape, her arms grew heavy at her sides, her skin condensed back onto her body, blood rush by blood rush. She stood in the centre of the room, coming together at the seams.

The next time Shurobhi came over, Ila's father's flat was a bustle of activity.

'What's going on?'

'My mother's coming over soon, with my aunt. They're taking me to a bride viewing.'

'Who's the bride?'

'Ami.'

Shurobhi's posture turned rigid. 'What? You've agreed to this?'

'Well, it's only a preliminary meeting,' she replied. 'You know, the one where you go to be inspected by your gnashing mother-in-law, who will say you're too fat and dark but she supposes she could train you into a decent housewife-type.'

'Is this a joke?'

'Nah,' Ila said, smiling. 'And I'm actually looking forward to it.'

Shurobhi stared at her, unable to say more.

Ila went on, 'I'll tell you what I know from his bio-data. He has a master's degree and a job in America. And his parents are worried because he's close to thirty and still unmarried.'

'Tall and fair too, I'm sure,' Shurobhi said, her lips twisting.

'Hard to tell from the photos, but promising… And Tahsin is next on the list, though I kind of wish it were his brother. Come, check out my outfit.'

Ila was determined not to let Shurobhi get her down. She couldn't tell her that what she really wanted was for time to just stop, so that she could stay where nothing had been decided, everything was to come, for better or for worse.

It was only in the car heading to Dhanmondi that Ila thought about how she might appear to Rox or Shurobhi, or any of their friends. They would find it absurd, even though these days, parental introductions followed by a period of dating were not uncommon. It was just the method of introduction that stood out here, replete with stiff families in starched outfits and arch commentary.

An hour and a half later, the five of them were still in the car, the traffic more jammed than usual. The driver and her mother were silent. Her aunt kept up a running monologue, which Ila had thought was relieving at first, but now found tiresome. Her father fidgeted in the front passenger seat. He interrupted his sister-in-law, his British accent clipping off the edges of his sentences. 'The house is on road eight, no? Shouldn't have come this way. Now we're late. Looks bad.'

'It's fine,' said her aunt. 'We get to be fashionably late. And they must understand the traffic. They live in this neighbourhood after all.' She eyed the immobile snake of cars with distaste.

Ila refrained from reminding her aunt that she herself had lived in this neighbourhood not too long ago. She twisted her crushed silk dupatta in her hands. Good thing she had picked a shalwar kameez with forgiving fabric for the car ride. Of course, her aunt had disapproved of the colour, saying the cerise was too dark for Ila's skin tone, but Shurobhi insisted it looked good. Ila thought so too.

Outside, the traffic thrummed and throbbed.

School had let out, and streams of laughing blue-pinafored girls were weaving between the cars. Braids of varying lengths and messiness swung past her window. She wished she were in high school again, when things weren't so complicated, when she was surer of what made sense. All the certainty from her conversations with Shurobhi faded. If there wasn't love to begin with, she had to count on it creating itself out of nothing. Could something like that see her through the rest of her life? Could it be deep enough, wide enough to contain her ridiculous, hopeful heart?

What if it weren't? What if they had children? At that time, would it matter if she'd gone for love or for reason? Did she really know anything about how the world worked, what it required? Were all the movies and the books so wrong about that missing piece – the love bit – that made you want to be part of the greater whirl, that seemed to solve everything in the beginning, but that Ila knew wouldn't solve anything in the end?

Why, she asked God silently, is it so hard to understand how to be happy?

By the time Ila walked into the flat on road eight, she was ready for anyone who showed even a trace of surety. Soon enough, she was enveloped by it. Her voluble aunt, his plainspoken mother, her sharp-tongued Nana who had insisted on taking a rickshaw on his own to meet them. Even the would-be groom, though he said little, seemed assured in his reserve. His eyes were direct, his lips full, his hands folded in his lap. She felt their gazes pulling at her, digging holes, leaving her in pieces that didn't quite add up to a whole.

Only her father seemed unsure, and Ila found herself gravitating towards him. Now, all the confidence seemed suspect, brimming the room with hot air, making it difficult to think. She needed to leave, and when she looked at her father, he knew this immediately. The meeting was brought to a close, a second one planned with an enthusiasm Ila found difficult to believe. How did the dour logistics of the conversation fade? Had the advent of parting sugarcoated the thought of their next connection?

She was startled when the boy appeared in front of her. Her Nana raised his voice in an attempt to create privacy. She found the act absurd and touching.

'Let's go for coffee soon,' he said. Ila could only nod. 'Could I have your mobile number?'

Ila fumbled for her phone and when she finally

retrieved it, she stared at it blankly. He took the phone from her hand and started entering his number. She was both piqued and relieved by his gesture, but said nothing. He gave it back to her, gently vibrating.

'Missed call from you to me,' he said, smiling easily, waving his own phone. 'I-L-A… is that right?' His tongue seemed to be testing the letters.

She watched his lips move in slow motion. She could do this, she thought, come to know that mouth, those hands, discover a different arrangement of her heart, one where the end wasn't in sight every beating moment.

'Yes,' she said at last, 'that's right.'

THE BEAUTY OF
BELONGING

there's only one thing that's left to miss
time (what's yours) time (what's mine)
the winter is digging its grave as I find
a way to see (show me)
to feel (tell me)
to stay

Any addict worth his sugar will tell you that you don't pick drugs to match your mood. I mean, you could try, but it's a hopeless task. Drugs, life, magic, God, sex, whatever you want to call it, figures when it will pick you up and where it will set you down.

I'm telling this pretty bit of junk to the girl that Dokkhin has brought around to mine. This one is too tall, but good looking, like all the rest. No lipstick, expressive hands. A black and white photograph. As long as she knows how to inhale, I don't care. Actually, Dokkhin's last paramour was sweet, though my ceiling got the best high ever with all the honey she let escape. You'd think there wasn't anyone left who didn't know how to suck a rolled-up bill. There was that girl in Cox's Bazaar who thought the Bong way was ghetto. Aluminium foil and lighters? We pop pills, she had drawled. Americans. No romance in their bones. And where's the love if it isn't in the going? When you're gone, you're gone after all. The beauty of belonging isn't that it lasts forever, but that you think it will.

Acid was the drug that taught me patience. You can't not stay in the now, on acid. It won't stop if you want it to. The present moment swells, neon stains the past, swallows the future whole.

Dokkhin's girl or friend, I think they met in college in the States, interrupts me. Or maybe she interrupted my train of thought. My blood is sped up enough that I can't remember whether I had been talking out loud or inside my head. Her name is Rox, and she's actually more than good looking. Her eyes glitter in this way that I can't take, so I avoid making eye contact. Why do some girls insist on boy mannerisms like arguing loudly? Though it means she's not shy, and I like not-shy. But then she asks me what my favourite drug is. Typical weekend partier question. As if it has anything to do with drugs.

I wish I were back in Cox. Next to the sea, wandering that strange symmetric forest. The summer I spent there, I filled up pad after pad with watercolour smears I thought were divine

at the time. Divine at the time. And I wonder
at the preciousness of my art. My sketchpads are
sitting in a box under my bed in Gulshan, probably
chewed up by insects and God knows what else
Bangladesh has cooked up for them. This country
is a black Goya world where humans are overrun.
There are creatures here not yet recorded in
insect history.

I didn't have a single visitor that Cox summer,
except for Dokkhin one hazy fortnight, when we
went through more pills than I can count. He
went into spasms in the end, and the sea turned
gunmetal in my mouth. I had warned him, but
that boy never understood the power of waiting.
He's like my brother Tahsin that way, only better
because he's not an ass-kissing self-serving prick
like the blood version.

When I got kicked out of my house, thanks
to you-know-who, it was Dokkhin who saved me,
found me a place to crash. I had just met him
at some fancy Dhaka do, and frankly, I hadn't
thought much. Far too well dressed, which only
meant he thought far too much about it all. An
Indian with impeccable manners, in Dhaka, for
a season of business. Fresh meat, thought the
scene. Freshly irritating, thought I. Until I met

him at the IC bar days later. I try not to go to these places, overrun as they are by expats or the Dhaka elite or sometimes, horrifyingly, both. Actually then, it's almost amusing, like watching two vapid and varied still-life scenes, each group stoic in their armours, jeans and shiny tops on one side, zealously ornamented saris on the other, glaring down each other's earnestly arrhythmic dance moves.

Anyhow, I needed a drink and my booze was tied up in the house I had just been expelled from. I called up a friend and got him to write me into the list. Sure, I have the foreign passport all good elites should, in my case, American, but I had never bothered to get a membership.

'Who needs drugs when your drug of choice is life?' That's the inane answer I give Rox in response to her inane question.

'People who have favourite drugs,' I elaborate gently, 'don't really know the point of drugs. They might not even know the point of life.'

But I can see now that the questions she's asking are not the aloud ones. They're the ones in her unbearable eyes. Fuck, where did Dokkhin find this one?

'Baltimore,' Dokkhin says, pouring himself

another dull gold tumbler of Black Label. He loves the stuff, though I can't understand why. It's what he drinks all the time. It was what he was drinking at the bar at the IC the night my kutta brother convinced my dad I needed tough love. I don't know why Tahsin cared about what I did. I wasn't working in garments, true, but I wasn't painting either, which he never thought was much of a hobby, let alone a profession. I was basically sleeping all day, staying up and out all night. He told our parents that throwing me out was the only thing that would teach me my ways. His ways rather. My mom, she nearly cried her eyes out. I'm the only one who can usually calm her down, but this time, I didn't. At first. But there was something hysterical about the way she was going on. So I tried to get her to stop, and that's when I realized that she was genuinely afraid for me. As if leaving home were some death knell. Foolish emotional woman.

Dokkhin agreed with me, though I realized soon after that Dokkhin tended to agree first and decide later. It was why the girls loved him so. It was why the girls hated him so. I, on the other hand, almost never say yes. Nor do I say no. I know it doesn't matter. It's all make-believe that we have any control over what happens in our lives. And I got tired of the lovecrush theatre of it long ago.

I didn't go to Cox that summer to paint, though that's what I tell everybody. They've all been waiting for my second exhibition, even though it's been years since my first, the one which exposed to me that delicate sewage flush of elitism. Serves me right though. I should have had the show in Bangladesh, not Brooklyn. But I was living in America, those heady post-college years where you think you actually run your own life because you can almost pay your rent. If you had to pay your rent, that is. I should have come back. Stopped living the hypocrisy sooner. Or at least brought the hypocrisy closer to home, closer to its centre. That way, the ignorant and loud-mouthed gallery gallivanters of Dhaka could have rightly pointed out the hackery I had produced.

I had been going straight then for a year, bound by an insane promise to Ila, and it was driving me dumb. Of course, my paintings followed my sinking lead, but none of the New Yorker hipster art-fucks had the balls to point it out. Instead, it was all *subversive talent, oil and water deconstructed, rewired and reverberant*, and other shit I can't deign to reproduce now. Every last one of my paintings went for some outrageous price. I reneged on each sale by giving my paintings away in Prospect Park one pastoral sunset, one by one, to whoever looked the longest.

I'll never paint again. But I won't tell anyone that because I know that never will always come back and rub itself all over your stupid face. The truth is, I went to Cox to escape Dhaka. Dhaka and its tired trinkery. Dhaka and its faded winter, its melodramatic summer. Dhaka drowning me in Ila's love. That's the real deal. I was running away from Ila. Oh yeah, she said she had nothing left to give me. But I know what she meant. That she had too much to give and it was spilling over my edges, costing her karmic energy by the second. That kind of talk kills me even though I know it's not all crap. Thankfully, Ila's voice is too deep to be anything but goddamn sexy. She could make me hard by reading me *Daily Star* headlines. True, it was the sports page and World Cup season, but still. 'Tigers Mauled!' and all the fucking rest, and there rose my desire under my kurta-pyjama.

The first time I saw Ila, she was wearing a grey shalwar kameez, wet from the rain, and I immediately wanted to fuck her. In that post-colonial, back-to-your-Tantric-roots, brown-erotica, woman-worshipping Western ways (no, I want you to come first), slipping into Eastern clothes (sorry, you were too much for me, premik, next time?).

The problem is that you can't love and leave too often with brown girls. Even if you leave their bodies flushed and pulsing, which I do, thank you very much. I'm not one of those boys. You can't fuck and run in Dhaka, but even in the mutinous underground bars of New York, you could get that rep. Whether or not you make it perfectly clear from the beginning that all you ever wanted was love, without the strings. It's the strings that fuck things up. Bind me to you, and I'll show you the surest path to flight.

'It's true,' Dokkhin tells me, 'but let's not talk about traps. Besides, we need more ice. Can you get some from your neighbour upstairs?'

'You're the one who needs more ice, bhai,' I say. 'I can't drink that shit, ice or no.'

'We can't all have your high-class tastes,' Dokkhin says, swigging the last of his whiskey.

'Fuck off, man,' I say. 'At least I knew what it was like to be middle class.'

We both laugh but we know who's older

money. Dokkhin's family is one of Kolkata's
bastions of wealth, going back generations. My
pop only made his money in the last couple of
decades. And seeing how my brother uses his
slimeball connections to grease things, I don't
know how long the cash will last. I believe in
karma as it turns out. One bad turn for another.

On my way back from the neighbour's, I stop
in the loo. Seems Rox doesn't believe in locking
doors. She's sitting on the toilet but waves me
in. I only need to shake out the ice crumbles at
the bottom of the bag into the sink, but when
I glance into the mirror, she's watching me. I
leave the bag in the sink and turn around. As I
lean down slowly, I can see her legs closing into
a dark velvet upside-down V. The oldest mystery
of them all. I have an urge to paint her. On her.
A tired O'Keefe image comes into my head. What
the bleeding edgers don't understand is that we
create those standard overdone images even
when there's something pure driving us. We do it
because of that purity. All the ways to jack it up,
splatter it, deconstruct it, build it back, they're
all just ways to get back to the original feeling, at
best; foils at worst. That's why 'I love you' means
something even now.

Ila was the first Bangali girl I loved. Hell, the first girl. Before that was a string of white girls. Even when I came back to Dhaka, it was easy finding them. A new crop of NGO-ers every season. But Ila, with her undulating curves and hair, got me for some reason. I couldn't stop touching her. I couldn't stop painting her. No drug ever felt as good. Drugs and Ila together would probably blow my mind, but for reasons both logistical and perhaps lucky, I never had the shot. When Ila found out about my habits, she got me to swear I'd never do anything when I was with her. At first, that was easy enough. But then it got harder. I saw Ila less. She doesn't realize it, but how often I see her means nothing. How little we talk means nothing. When she's around, the world shrinks and fits into my heart. When I'm gone, my heart shrinks and disappears into the world.

The bathroom window is open and a breeze flicks at me. I'm so close to Rox that I can squint the glitter of her eyes into pinprick stars, growing, falling, fading. A living painting. Or is it a painted life? I clap suddenly between her legs and look at my hands. Fucking mosquito. Black ink fairy imprint across my palms. I grab the bag of ice and bang out of the bathroom.

Every moment that ticks in this time line of us, it lasts forever, or a day. So when I come back into the room, it's as if I never left. It's as if I'm coming in for the first time. I freeze, as I sometimes have to when the two realities coincide.

'Welcome.' Dokkhin smiles. 'Or is it welcome back?'

I have long since stopped being surprised at his knowing. I know my internal monologue's fucked sometimes. As in, I don't know when it's internal and when it's aloud. But even when I've made a ludicrous leap of imagination, Dokkhin somehow follows.

When Rox enters, she goes straight to Dokkhin's side and sits neatly beside him as if bidden. The room seems darker so I can't see her eyes anymore, thank God. Dokkhin seems oblivious. He's in the Matrix, working the strip of aluminium foil, pressing it, stretching it, running the lighter flame along it. When he's placed the little red pill on the edge of the aluminium, he hands me the lighter. For all his suave ways, Dokkhin can't keep a lighter lit while he inhales so I always do the honours. The rolled-up 100-taka note is sitting on a box of cigarettes. He puts it in his mouth and waits as I hold the lighter under the silver strip. A second later, a tendril of smoke is born. As it widens and wends, Dokkhin's breath calls to it. I trace the lighter under the path of the pill as it smokes and slides down the strip.

The smoke is now entering me, that familiar metallic tang girding my lungs. Rox's whole body, not just her eyes, in darkness now. Dokkhin a silhouette, then a shadow, then nothing.

I am alone. As I breathe, each rib contracts under my muscles, under my skin. I can see the building of my Cubist body. It slowly becomes. Fuck, there is nothing like it. This understanding of why we are. This salience of being, itself a reason. It's why I still pop, inhale, shoot, chew, lick, snort, suck, absorb all of it, despite the steel pincers flexing on my brain some nights, most nights, every night.

I know what I have to do. The thing that always belonged to me. The way anything belongs to you in the moment you engage. I pick up my paintbrush.

A second later, a lifetime later, I feel Dokkhin shaking me. His voice fades in and out like a pirated soundtrack. He's telling me something absurd. He's telling me not to die. Ila wavers like a flame into my candlewax mind, midnight skin and midnight hair. I'm not in my room anymore. A bumper car world resolves. It grumbles and shakes around me. It pixelates. Fluorescence in my eyes. Ila wavers out.

STAY

who are we, he asked
lovers, she said
to his wrinkling nose
it's not enough, he replied
not even close

The red glow of the lights inside the Princeton Club made everything seem both high and low class all at once. Of course the patrons were high class. Hardly anyone in the South Kolkata bars wasn't, but those at the Princeton Club were bearable only in their indifference to everything but the cheap drinks. That's why he had picked this place for their meeting. He knew she'd be late and he wanted to be able to pay for his drinks while he waited. He lit another cigarette and caught himself coughing in anticipation. Clearing room in his lungs, he thought to himself ruefully and laughed.

'Dada, arekta Kingfisher,' he asked the reluctant waiter who was probably hoping for a more interesting customer. He'd be rewarded when Rox showed up with her flair. There was something about her that never failed to look foreign. No matter where she was or what she wore. He was sure it would be the same now, though he hadn't seen her in years. It was the only thing he was sure of about her. Everything else was up for grabs.

He had forgotten about her when she came up behind him. He had been lost in thought about his new short, a meditative aural experiment. His idea was that the audience be challenged with sound, to notice its presence, its absence, its power. He had been shooting in Ballygange for two days now with a crew of two dozen, including one precocious brat of a child actor. There was something about using kids in films that felt like cheating to him. The scene only had to start and the boy's earnestness took care of the rest. No, it was more like integrity than earnestness, a hyper-accessible and inevitable leap from thought to action. Of course, an audience would accept a child's actions and motives. Wasn't that the definition of a child – purity of intention? It was one of his goals to elicit that reaction from an audience, but about a seriously unreliable adult character.

'Arul,' Rox said in his ear. Her hand cupped the back of his head. He put his glass down on the warped wood bar and turned. She was thinner, more angular than before. His arm slipped around her waist, as her skin offered itself to his hands. Was it always going to be like this? That first split second of drowning in her smell?

'Let me look at you,' he said, pushing her away from him. She withdrew in amusement. Did she know what he was thinking? No, he decided. It was just Rox's way to always look as if she did. Besides, he had no desire to rekindle their affair, no matter what his body thought. It had been torture, their breaking up, though she had never guessed. She had imagined herself the only casualty in that war, as the starry ones often do. True, his fade to a shadow of himself had probably not lasted any longer than her gloryburst of grief, but her stamp on his life was a wound he still treasured a decade later.

She took his hand and pressed it into his chest, curling her wrist in a familiar gesture, her knuckles against his heart.

'It's good to see you,' she said.

Her eyes were even brighter than he remembered. She was wearing a long cotton kurta and jeans. The kurta was thin enough that he could see the silhouette of her torso through it, her breasts the same magnificent same.

'You're here for a week, right?' he said suddenly.

'I am,' she said.

'Would you be in my new short?' he asked.

'No,' she said, just as promptly, 'but I want to invite you to dinner. Come.'

'Where?' he said, letting himself be pulled along. It was like this with Rox. You just got swallowed into her orbit.

'You tell me.'

He could never tell when Rox was being real. She claimed it was all the time, but he didn't quite believe it. The last time he had seen her was a few years ago. He had moved back to India after graduation and she had come to Mumbai for work. They had both been in between relationships and she had been obviously wanting. He hadn't known why he had (mostly) denied her. It was impossible to completely deny her. She exuded something that was unabashedly sexual, but in a way that was without guile. The physical was, for her, something separate from emotional. Or perhaps an extension of her (often) platonic affection.

But he couldn't touch Rox without feeling something that went beyond the physical. Or maybe that was just his loneliness trying to make meaning out of nothing. Shamtoli, his last girlfriend, had got under his skin. She had made a project out of their relationship and, having helped him get in on a sweet production gig, had promptly moved onto her next mission. But the year he had spent with her in his tiny Jadavpur flat had proved his most adult romantic encounter. He was still angry at his feeling of loss.

'Dokkhin is meeting us,' Rox informed him.

'Even though he's getting married in three days?' he asked with genuine pleasure. 'Is he still living in Bangladesh?'

'He is. I actually saw him a couple times in Dhaka. I was just there for Ila's wedding.'

'Ila got married!' Arul said. 'Not very punk rebel of her. Or did she marry a woman?'

The thought apparently gave Rox pause for a second, and then she smiled. 'No, she married Tahsin, a proper Bangladeshi boy from a good family and all. But of course, knowing Ila, she scandalized everyone by dating his addict brother first. I met them both. The brother, Oyon, was a good friend of Dokkhin's actually. Anyway, apparently her husband is a forgiving man.'

Arul shook his head. 'Good, because wild streaks don't go away that easily.'

'She's not that wild really. I could see what she

saw in his brother. He's an incredible artist, and despite his craziness, he seemed kind of brashly real.'

'Where are you staying in Cal anyway?' Arul wondered if he should ask her to stay at his, though he didn't think it would be a good idea.

'At the Tolly,' she said.

'Really? The Tolly?' he asked. It was his turn to be amused, though he knew Rox had moved past their days of bread and cheese for breakfast, lunch, and dinner. In their university days in Maryland, they would often surprise each other with little additions to their 'gora' meals as they called them, more for the pale shade of the food than the race of people. Bags of potato chips, popcorn, rolls of cookie dough on special occasions.

'Dokkhin got the room for me.' She grinned in acknowledgement. Rox looked high class, even though she hadn't grown up that way. Her parents still lived in a squashed three-bedroom rowhouse in North Baltimore, and she and her brother had worked since they were teenagers. But there was something about her bearing, the set of her jaw. And she didn't give a shit about class, which was the only reason he had said yes when she first asked him out. They had been at a party at

Dokkhin's sprawling College Park flat, his third year, her first, embroiled in a heated argument about globalization, a topic cutting through both her healthcare and his politics courses. Suddenly, Rox had interrupted herself.

'Can I ask you something?' she had said a bit hesitantly.

'Of course,' he had replied, wondering at her change of mood. Had he been his usual overbearing self and offended her as he did almost everyone?

She had swallowed the rest of her beer in a deliberate and disarming motion and asked him out. He had been so taken aback he hadn't said anything at first. It would be the first of many times he would wonder how she could switch topics so quickly. Had she really been invested in the earlier conversation? How could she be so intense one moment and then laugh so quickly another?

'Conversational genius,' Dokkhin proclaimed. 'All Bengalis have it.'

'Or we're essentially fickle,' Rox would add with utmost sincerity.

But Rox was different this time. She wasn't being careful or restrained, but she was taking more time with her responses. Surprisingly, it was making him more reckless. More drawn to her. Was it another Rox plot? He wondered, and immediately felt guilty for ascribing subterfuge to her actions.

'I think Dokkhin will crash in my room at the Tolly tonight. You should too,' she said.

'Like old times,' he said, and they both laughed. The last time all three of them had been together was when they were all in university in America. Dokkhin would stop by their noisy off-campus studio, late at night, at any inopportune moment, but it had never mattered. Both Rox and he liked Dokkhin tremendously, and they would invariably end up getting drunk on Dokkhin's whiskey and talking into the night.

Arul decided they would eat at Dhaba, a crowded Ballygange joint with fluorescent lighting and greasy irresistible rolls. Dokkhin came straight from the airport in a battered white Ambassador and joined them. He entered with his usual understated energy and hugged both Rox and him for a long time. Then, taking Rox's hand, he assailed Arul with a barrage of questions about film-making. Dokkhin came from money and there was never any doubt that he would continue the tradition. Much to his family's dismay, he had refused to take over his father's highly successful electronics company. Instead, he had gone off to Dhaka on a mint garment industry deal. But he never spoke more than a disparaging sentence or two about his work. What he was interested in was everything else. Art, politics, war, literature, women, anything but business.

They were soon having a spirited discussion about the making and selling of film. What was the point of art? Was it to provoke intellectual response through emotional means or vice versa, or something else altogether? What about Arul's impulse to ignore both intellectual and emotional space and focus on the senses instead? Love, said Rox. Justice, said Dokkhin. Touching, Arul thought. The most primal sense of all.

Since he had no way of reaching his audience that way using film, he was playing with sound, the second-most integral sense in his opinion. The structure of his latest film had stayed close to his original storyboards, but because of the boy, something fundamental was different. Or maybe he was imagining the disconnect. Either way, seeing the film later had the effect of watching someone else's vision. No matter that he had micromanaged every angle and shadow. He wondered if it was the same for everyone. He knew some directors couldn't watch their completed films easily. Others, like him, scavenged every frame. Was anyone happy?

Despite Dokkhin's looming nuptials, he had not spoken of it or his fiancée, nor had he let go of Rox's hand for a moment. His perfectly manicured nails pressed into the centre of her palm, and Arul watched the faint half moons turn white and disappear. But Rox seemed oblivious to everything but their roller-coaster conversation. Should the non-profit model give way to for-profit social business? Was candid photography a high art form? Would Arul ever stop wearing cargo pants?

Since Dokkhin was always prepared, he had a bottle of whiskey, his toxin of choice. Many hours and a bottle and taxi ride later, they stumbled into a lux white-sheeted hotel room at the Tolly. Within moments, Dokkhin was sprawled on the king-size bed, fully clothed and sound asleep. Arul followed Rox into the bathroom where she was brushing her teeth. She looked at him in the mirror, her mouth full of foam. He put down the toilet seat lid and sat down on it. She spit and rinsed and turned and leaned against the counter. Her kurta was incompletely tucked into the bottom edge of her bra, an old bathroom habit of hers. Her stomach stretched tantalizingly down into her jeans.

'How are you?' she asked.

'How aren't you?' he countered. This line of Rumi's had been their favourite ironic rejoinder.

'That bad?' she said, smiling. 'I heard you broke up with someone recently.'

He realized he had not thought of Shamtoli once that evening. That his anger had somehow dissipated. That all he could think of now was Rox. He pulled her body against him, smelling her skin. Her hands curled around his ears and then linked around his neck. He sat her down on his lap, facing him, and pressed his mouth against hers. She kept her mouth closed. He waited, as their eyelashes tangled, her nose brushing past his cheekbone. She started smiling slowly, the corners of her lips widening against his face, and then finally pursing, gathering, opening. He thought he had forgotten the taste of her tongue but realized, in that moment, that it was a memory that would never leave him. It was part of his sensory understanding of intimacy.

On the set of his film, the little boy had arranged two armies of different-sized stones on the uneven sidewalk. An unusually smooth black stone was the general of one army. In between takes, the boy kept resetting the fallen soldiers because of some conflicted desire for symmetry, or what Arul imagined as fairness, or what Rox would describe as empathy. He kissed Rox again, for once thinking of nothing, not felled armies, not even himself.

The sound of his mobile phone jangling woke Arul in the morning. He untangled himself from the silky cotton sheets and leapt up to answer it. As he spoke to his production manager in a low hoarse voice, he peered through the paisley brocade curtains at the green expanse of lawn outside. The light burned into his aching vision. He dropped the heavy cloth quickly and turned back to the darkened room.

Was that Dokkhin's hand on Rox's hip? His other arm wrapped like a tentacle under and around her? Arul closed his eyes and let the feeling wash over him. It wasn't just jealousy or possessiveness, feelings that, until yesterday, had been bound to his thoughts about Shamtoli. It was a lightning understanding of something deeper, that he could be with one person for the rest of his life, that he wanted the same.

It was true he could have been rebounding from his lost love with Shamtoli, misunderstanding his renewed ability to feel, with this overwhelming sense of commitment. But it was also true that he had never felt more free, more desolate than in this moment. He opened his eyes and looked at Rox, stone general, bent on her glistering desires. He admired her love, the kind that never seemed to dim in intensity, no matter how far and wide she sent it. His affection was less generous, weakening when shared, zero-sum game. Perhaps this was his test. Rox was his unreliable character, but with enough integrity to fill a life. And Arul was the audience. Would he buy in? Would he stay? He shook his head.

The marblelized floor of the bathroom was cold and incompletely covered with plush towels. He pulled on his crumpled shirt, shivering a little, sliding his feet into broken-down pumas.

Rox made a sighing sound and he stilled. He walked back to the bed silently and stood over her. Just then, she opened her eyes and looked at him. Her gaze was neither curious nor passive. Only keenly aware.

Arul had the sensation that he had always been standing there. That this waking moment would last forever. He reached down and touched her face. Legion, this sense, touch. This much was true.

HIGH WATER

Pilar is walking
7 times around the fire
once each, she counts
for the 7 years
she's been with Gabriel
but that was in the east of Spain
this is the south of India
a very different
planet

They say the sea is high today. One of the drivers was late. The cook never showed. Gabriel's wedding outfit has been carefully pressed and is lying on his neatly made four-poster bed. He's not sure how they do it, but he never manages to catch the maids fixing his room. Every morning, he emerges from the bathroom after brushing and shaving to find it all done, even underwear neatly folded. He wants to watch the voluptuous Bengali maid make his bed. Her name is July, which he finds lovely though everyone else in the family laughs at the proviciality of naming someone after the month she was born in. What about Abril? Maig?

Juny? Did no one except July's mother want to go further in time?

He wonders how Pilar is doing. His mother is in charge of her getting ready and he doesn't envy his bride-to-be. Amma was a stern enough taskmaster but with something as important as her son's marriage, she has increased her threat level to orange, as his brother Sailan would say. Maybe even red. Of course, Sailan's wedding had been as pompous an affair as possible. It is only Gabriel's repeated request that has kept his own celebration relatively simple. No mehendi party, no ring ceremony, no post banquet or three. Only a wedding ceremony, shortened to a mere three hours, and a reception immediately following.

'Done in a day,' he had whispered to Pilar when they stepped off the plane into the hot windy air.

'I thought you said it was winter here,' Pilar had replied, flushing pink immediately. Despite her Mediterranean birth, she has never done well in the sun. She loves the heat, but too much time outdoors and she turns a radish red. Gabriel laughed at her words, although he had expected cooler weather too. He has been to Chennai only twice before, once as a teenager, and once as an

adult for a frantic week of festivities for Sailan's
wedding. Since neither heat nor cold bothers him
much, he hadn't noticed the weather either time.

'Pilar will love it, the ceremony of it, and
with that pale skin, she'll look beautiful in our
colours,' Dr Mrs Deva had said in one of her
more persuasive arguments. She usually reserves
her cajoling for her older son, as Sailan responds
badly to anything else. While Gabriel dislikes her
semi-threats probably as much as his brother does,
he is less likely to respond in kind. Still, it took
months for him to give in to her demands for a
Tamil Brahmin marriage ceremony. His father had
been no help in the matter, despite understanding
Gabriel's position profoundly. He had exhausted
his ire well before Sailan's lush and exorbitant
affair, and has assigned himself a non-functioning
role in all successive marital events.

> who'd have thought
> a wedding in India
> could be like a rave
> in the Mediterranean?
> Pilar is painted up as richly
> colour laved onto her eyelids
> each time she blinks
> a heavy curtain of copper
> disappears the water blue of her irises

They are all staying in his maternal grandparents' sprawling house in Mahalingapuram. After growing up in his parents' cramped house, and his even closer quarters with Pilar, it seems a luxury, all the empty rooms filled now with their suitcases and jetlagged bodies. Gabriel is surprised to find how gently spoken his grandparents are. He had imagined versions of his mother, assured and aggressive, but with a more conservative bent and thicker accents. Instead, it's with quiet feeling that they welcome both him and Pilar, making him think that perhaps having a proper Indian wedding wasn't such a bad decision after all.

Gabriel starts putting on his clothes when there is a knock on the door. July enters without waiting for an answer. She has a perfectly round face, a closely clothed body. Faced with Gabriel's naked body, she flees without a word, the door banging shut behind her. He starts laughing, partly in embarrassment. In the dim light, the outline of his body is sketched in the mirror. Years of windsurfing have carved out his shoulders, his thighs, his arms, narrowed his waist, compacted his torso. He's shaved his beard for the first time in years. It makes him look at least a decade younger, barely adult. Pilar loves his beard, but when she saw him yesterday, bare faced, she had touched his lips wonderingly, immediately arousing him.

'I had forgotten what your mouth looked like,' she had whispered to him.

'What did you do to that poor maid?' Sailan pushes open the door. 'Oh, I see.' He comes in and closes the door. 'You could lock the door, but I suppose that wouldn't suit your exhibitionist tendencies.'

Gabriel grins and turns back to his clothes. 'It's good you're here, because I'm not quite sure how this dhoti thing works.' He hands the white silk fabric to his brother. The gold border along the edge matches the lustrous kurta lying on the bed.

'How did you crumple it already?' Sailan takes the dhoti from him and shakes it out. 'And I have no fucking clue how it's worn either. I'll get Appa. But for goodness sake, put on some underwear.'

> despite Pilar's geisha-pale skin
> the make-up artist has caked on Clinique
> mehndi stains her hands and feet
> she feels like negative space
> her skin showing through
> in between the patterns
> the tips of her fingers
> black and pungent

Their procession of cars is five strong. Gabriel and Pilar are in different cars, with one of Gabriel's parents in each. Gabriel's mother has instructed Sailan's wife, Monica, to ride with her and Pilar. Gabriel is glad because he never got on with his sister-in-law. She has a hold over his brother he doesn't understand. It's hard to get through to Sailan; his veneer is watertight, bullet-proof. But one pitched tone from Monica and he dissolves into a pleading mess. However, Gabriel is overjoyed to see his five-year-old niece, Vani, bullet into the backseat with him, despite Monica's call. Vani settles into his lap and starts stroking his face.

'Your beard is gone!' she says in her arch American English, enunciating like a school teacher.

'No t'agrada, señorita?' he asks deferentially. 'I saved some of the hair. I can try pasting it back on if you like.' He starts rummaging around in his pockets and she squeals with disgust.

'Come here, reina,' Sailan says, pulling Vani into his lap. 'You're crushing your uncle's wedding outfit.'

She reluctantly acquiesces and then is absorbed by the outside. Neither Gabriel nor her father is of any help in explaining much of what is

scrolling past their windows, but their pace is slow
enough that she is able to get a good look at each
animal, human and contraption that passes by.

'It's a parade!' she cries out, as a palanquin
held up by six men passes by, containing a veiled
icon. But trailing the procession is the sound of
wailing. Gabriel rolls down the window and has
the sensation of a record player playing five tracks
at once. Inside that clamour, there is something
in the air, some high-wire tension, a waiting act,
queer silence despite the bustle. The sides of the
road are lined with streams of people walking single
file. Some are determined, some lost. A woman
sits on the roadside, her eyes wide and shocked,
her limbs draped about her as loosely as her sari.

'What is it?' Gabriel asks. 'What is happening?'

'Close your window,' is Sailan's only response,
but Gabriel can hear a note of uncertainty in the
gentleness of his command. He leaves the window
open, and Sailan doesn't say anything more.

> the Hindu priest could be
> like an Ibiza DJ
> smiling from the corner
> conducting the crowd at her whim
> chants Gabriel's mother has explained
> so carefully, so uselessly

The last time Gabriel had seen his brother was when Sailan had come to Barcelona from New York with Monica and Vani. Gabriel had insisted they stay with him at least one night, if only to give him time with Vani, and perhaps fit in some windsurfing with Sailan. Pilar and he had given up their tiny bedroom to their guests, and slept on the lumpy living-room futon. In the morning, Pilar had unexpectedly roused herself early to make breakfast. She usually never woke before noon since she worked the night shift as a restaurant chef. He had woken to the clanking of pots and running water. Since their flat was so small, he only had to open his eyes to see where she was. She was at the kitchen counter, chopping and dicing in her lightning way, wearing the slinky blue nightgown he had got her last year. Her shoulder bones stuck out between the spaghetti straps, her skin translucent with blue veins, her brown hair tousled.

He placed the flat of his hand in between the wings of her shoulders, as always marvelling at the difference in their skin colours, Pilar pale and freckled, Gabriel dark from the decades he has spent in the sun since childhood, on the football fields, at the docks, with the sea.

They had had a rowdy breakfast followed by a long walk on the boardwalk in Barceloneta. In the afternoon, Gabriel and Sailan had gone windsurfing, although the wind had been a bit on the strong side. Pilar and Monica had found common ground in their love for shoes and had dragged Vani around Plaza Catalunya. It was possibly the best time Gabriel had ever had with his brother and his family, but he wasn't sure it would happen again. Towards the end, Vani had come down with a cold, turning Monica irritable. Both had kept Sailan close by with numerous requests. Gabriel didn't know whether either of them had very good memories of their time in Spain.

the scent of flowers is so strong
bound up in her slipslippy hair
she feels faint
from the fragrance

so fine, cries the hairdresser
so thin, she means, Pilar thinks
the hairdresser's own hair
shampoo commercial worthy

It is only after the wedding, when their cavalry of cars has fought the crowds back to the city, after they have driven into the dusty green neighbourhood where his grandparents live, slid past the wrought-iron gate of their compound, pushed open the heavy wooden door to the house, skirted past the mysterious stacks and bundles someone has left in the foyer, settled into the over-large living room with the under-sized TV, that they start to understand.

High water. Gabriel cannot match the images on the screen, the furiously yawing ocean, with his memory of the mild Mediterranean sea. He has grown up a water baby, the ebb and flow of the tide more familiar ground than ground itself. But even on its worst days, when the wind conspires with water against everything that dares to ride it, the Med has never looked like this.

Gabriel leaves his family standing, sitting, open-mouthed, tight-lipped, silent, watching. He goes out to the back garden to smoke. The gold band tightens around his finger as he strikes a match. He's now officially married, on the day of a tsunami. Does it mean something? Pilar and he have been together for how long now? Since he took that Barceloneta dock management post, the job his parents hate to admit their son has. A boat herder, Monica had called it once.

He doesn't understand what his brother sees in his wife. She is beautiful, of course. She has to be because Sailan always had a thing for pretty faces. She's smart too, having scratched up the money for her own consulting company and built it into a tiny powerhouse on Fifth Avenue. But she has a harsh American manner, and seems innately unhappy with her lot, determined that everyone follow her miserable lead.

Perhaps it's the sex, Gabriel thinks, as the smoke fills his lungs, clearing his head. Perhaps Monica gives the best head with that pouty mouth. He imagines his proud sister-in-law on her knees in front of his brother, then in front of him.

they cross a cloud of incense
and Pilar struggles not to cough
or itch her forehead
as she remembers the tikli
delicate as a gold hammer
banging the ivory nail
of her forehead

Grey air exits his body into the twilight. His grandfather's garden – it's not his grandmother who is responsible for the chaotic and colourful planting – is becoming a skyline silhouette of clumpy bushes, rangy trees. But something is wrong. Someone is weeping in the garden, behind the ramshackle betel nut tree crowded with crows. Gabriel walks along the dirt footpath and stops by the tree. It's July and she is crying harder than he's ever seen anyone cry. He crouches beside her, listening to her words float into haphazard sentences.

'The water was everywhere, I wasn't there, I was here, I was working, then I heard about the sea, it was rising, and my child was still home, so I ran, I ran back, the dogs were all gone, I saw them leaving in the morning, they all left with me, barking madly, running, I didn't understand why, but they did, the dogs, they knew about the water, now I can't find her, my child, my baby, Anjon, the water was so high, I looked all day, and still I cannot find her, my baby, she can barely walk yet, but I can't find her, my hut was still there, barely standing, full of water, full of rubbish, I found, I found my mother's bangles, the only thing I have left from Bangladesh, my baby, my baby, I have lost my baby, I have lost everything now, it cannot be, I cannot, I cannot be.'

July's Tamil is broken, simple enough that Gabriel can understand what she's saying though

he knows anyone would have understood the grief
in her voice.

'What would you have me do?' he asks gently,
touching her shoulder. Her tunic is thin and soft.

She looks up at him, her eyes so swollen they
are almost shut. 'Find her.'

'Come,' he says, holding out his hand.

He finds two large flashlights in a kitchen
cupboard and then they hire an auto to take
them to the sea. The last time he was here, eight
years ago for Sailan's wedding, the beach was
filled, vibrant. Evening strollers, pani puri carts,
the sugarcane machine, targets made of coloured
balloons, a creaking merry-go-round.

Now, in the impossible dark, everything is
different. Gabriel's sandals disappear into the
mud immediately, and he leaves them. The
arcs of their flashlights sweep uselessly over the
tree branches, the dead fish, the wavy panes of
tin, the plastic sheets, the rotting rubbish, and
everywhere, the mud and the water. The stench
is overwhelming, the smell blowing in and away
and in again. Each minute Gabriel feels he can't
go on, his feet cut up by the debris, his muscles
aching, he shines his light on July, and then
cannot bring himself to say anything. To his

relief, it's her flashlight that gives out first, his half an hour later.

In the morning, they return to the beach with Pilar. As they arrive, Gabriel feels Pilar's hope draining, her grip on his arm tight. There is a calm in the sky that belies the destruction below. Even the sea looks as if it's lying down, stretching under the sun. July's face is impassive. She begins at her hut and moves in widening concentric circles. Gabriel's feet feel raw inside his new sandals and he walks slowly towards the hut. A twisted rope of palm-leaf fibre lies like a snake in the doorway. He steps over it, directly into a thick pool of slime.

'Merda,' he whispers.

'Sí, és cert,' Pilar whispers back. 'It's what it is.' He looks at her sharply and she turns away and follows July's spiral.

The roof sags above Gabriel's head and he crouches down and closes his eyes. His pants soak into the sludge, the sludge onto his skin. He breathes in, willing his goosebumps to retract. He breathes out. Still, his body rebels. *In*. The baby is alive. *Out*. The baby is dead. *In*. She is alive. *Out*. She is dead. *In*. I am alive. *Out*. I am dead. *In*. Alive. *Out*. Dead. *In*. *Out*.

It is then that he feels the ocean speaking, the

way he has all his life, the way he has heard it from his earliest remembered dreams. The tide pulls him to understanding, and then pushes him away.

> they stop directly in the line of smoke
> her water-blue eyes watering
> she catches Gabriel's gaze
> clouded and mischievous
> I'm doing this for you
> she tells him silently
> don't you forget

On the day Gabriel is leaving India, he goes back to the ocean. The sea is rough and noisy and, for the first time in his life, the sound rankles. He automatically walks towards July's hut. The ruin has been cleared from the front and a folded sari hangs in the doorway. He steps in and the fabric swings into place behind him. The darkness swallows his senses, and he barely flinches when a hand reaches up to him from the damp ground. When his palms brush past her face, he can feel that she has not yet stopped crying, that she never might.

'I have no one,' she whispers. 'I have no one. My baby is gone.'

'Where is your baby's father?' he asks.

'He left before Anjon was born. It is a just punishment. I know. Because I left my children in Bangladesh. I ran away. Only my sister knows what terrible things I've done. Even she may never forgive me.'

'Where is your sister? Why don't you go to her?'

'I have no way of going home,' she says dully, her grasp loosening.

'I'll give you a way,' he says, catching her, pressing her languid body against himself.

'Don't let me go,' she says then, her voice breaking. 'Don't leave me.'

Gabriel holds her, his hands touching each part of her body, one by one, as if by doing so, he might connect her into a whole. Her arms to her elbows. Her shoulders to her throat to her face. Her breasts to her waist to her hips. Her knees to her ankles to her feet. He encloses her rigid fingers in his hands, presses them to his heart.

When he leaves, July is sleeping. He empties his wallet, tens of thousands of rupees, wads it under her soft clothes.

I am not letting go, he tells her as he steps, backwards, out of the hut. The light rushes in and falls upon her body. I am not leaving.

ACKNOWLEDGEMENTS

Thank you to the editors of the publications in which these stories appeared previously, sometimes in different forms.

'The Straight Path' was published in *The Daily Star Book of Bangladeshi Writing*, edited by Khademul Islam, *Daily Star*, Bangladesh (2006), and anthologized in *The New Anthem: The Subcontinent in Its Own Words*, edited by Ahmede Hussain, Tranquebar, India (2009).

'Now Go' was published in *580 Split*, USA (Spring 2006).

'The Alphabet Game' was published in *Sliptongue*, USA (Early Autumn 2006).

'Stay' was published in *SN Review* (Winter 2007), and reprinted in the *Daily Star* newspaper in Bangladesh (30 June 2007).

'Before You Eat' was published in the *Daily Star* newspaper in Bangladesh (27 January 2007), reprinted in Scroll.in (15 November 2014), and a 600-word excerpt was selected as a Highly Commended Winner in the Commonwealth Broadcasting Association's 2011 Short Story Contest, UK.

'The Beauty of Belonging' was published in the *Daily Star* newspaper in Bangladesh (15 September 2007).

'High Water' was published in the *Farallon Review*, USA (March 2008).

'Wax Doll' was published in the *Daily Star* newspaper in Bangladesh (May 24, 2008), and anthologized in *Lifelines: New Bangladeshi Writing*, edited by Farah Ghuznavi, Zubaan Books, India (2012).

'Alo' was published in *Gander Press*, USA (September 2008).

Thank you to the Fulbright Scholars Program for giving me my first taste of 100 per cent art-making time, and for my extraordinary stay in Bangladesh and India. To Somak, for that first letter, moral support to keep writing. To Khadem, who encouraged and published my work from the beginning. To the first readers of my first fiction: Ram, Mahmud, Mary, Chellis, and always already

Simi. To Josh, for all the joyful support. To Sheba, who walks with me. To Alan, the stalwart, despite the continents between us. To Baby, of the big heart and everlasting spirit. To Sabrina Aunty, who is my tribe in every sense of the word. And to my parents, for loving and never leaving.

About the Author

Abeer Y. Hoque is a Bangladeshi American writer and photographer, born in Nigeria. *The Lovers and the Leavers* is her first book of fiction. She has a book of travel photographs and poems, *The Long Way Home*, and her memoir, *Olive Witch*, is forthcoming from HarperCollins *Publishers* India.

Hoque is the recipient of a 2007 Fulbright Scholarship, among several other writing fellowships. Her writing and photography have been published in *Guernica*, *Outlook Traveller*, *India Today*, and *The Daily Star*. She has degrees from the University of Pennsylvania's Wharton School of Business and an MFA in writing from the University of San Francisco. She lives in New York City.

For more information, visit olivewitch.com.

3rd Jan
Friday at noon

2255 Ignacio Valley

Suit W 2nd Fl.

925-378-4884